KT-196-016

PAW

WITHDRAWN

Please return on or before the latest date above.
You can renew online at *www.kent.gov.uk/libs*
or by telephone 08458 247 200

H9

C155358672

THE RANCHER'S UNEXPECTED FAMILY

THE RANCHER'S UNEXPECTED FAMILY

BY

MYRNA MACKENZIE

First published in Great Britain 2012
by Mills & Boon, an imprint of Harlequin (UK) Limited.
Large Print edition 2013
Harlequin (UK) Limited, Eton House,
18-24 Paradise Road, Richmond, Surrey TW9 1SR

© Harlequin Books S.A. 2012

ISBN: 978 0 263 23164 9

Special thanks and acknowledgement are given
to Myrna Mackenzie for her contribution to
THE LARKVILLE LEGACY series.

Harlequin (UK) policy is to use papers that are natural,
renewable and recyclable products and made from
wood grown in sustainable forests. The logging and
manufacturing process conform to the legal environmental
regulations of the country of origin.

Printed and bound in Great Britain
by CPI Antony Rowe, Chippenham, Wiltshire

CHAPTER ONE

KATHRYN ELLIS closed her eyes and took a deep breath. What she was about to do, seeking out Holt Calhoun when he clearly didn't want to be found…

She swallowed hard. It had been years since she'd seen him and she tried not to envision Holt with his dark good looks and those brown eyes flecked with gold that pinned a person to a wall. The fact that she had once wanted those eyes to pin her, anywhere, was beside the point. She'd been young and naive enough not to understand what she was asking for then. Now she was older, a bit battered and not nearly as naive. She'd learned that a forceful, controlling man was the worst kind of nightmare for a woman like her.

Yet she was voluntarily walking right into the lion's den.

"So walk," she whispered as she climbed from

her barely-held-together car and started toward Holt's family home on the Double Bar C Ranch. During the few years she'd lived here, she had driven past the ranch and seen the big white house in the distance but she'd never been inside…or even on the grounds. She'd wanted to be invited in back when she'd been a teenager and called Larkville home. Now she didn't.

But she was going in anyway.

Her heartbeat thudding in her throat, she rang the doorbell and waited, willing herself to stay strong, stand tall, look professional.

But the baby kicked at that moment, and despite the fact that she should be used to such things by now, she splayed one hand over her abdomen and glanced down.

The door opened and she jumped. To her relief and regret, it wasn't Holt but Nancy Griffith, his housekeeper. The woman had kind eyes, but right now she looked a bit concerned.

"I'm sorry. I didn't call ahead, but—" Kathryn cleared her throat, trying not to sound nervous "—is Holt around?"

Nancy smiled at her. "I'm afraid he's not. Since

he returned from, well, I guess everybody knows where he was."

I don't, Kathryn thought. Because she had been determined not to be one bit curious about Holt's personal life. *No doubt a woman had been involved,* Kathryn couldn't help thinking. Holt had always had women trailing after him.

"But he's home now, right?" she asked. "I'd heard that he'd returned."

"He's home, but he's not here. Since he came back, he's been so tied up in the office that today he declared he was getting out on the range and nothing was going to stop him."

Including me, Kathryn thought. She'd tried to call Holt several times this week, even this morning. He hadn't picked up. Nor had he replied to her requests for an appointment to see him. She was pretty sure that he knew what she wanted. Maybe he'd heard about it from the mayor. Clearly, he wasn't enthused. She'd been warned not to expect much.

She didn't expect *anything,* but she wanted—

No. Don't go there, she ordered herself. Wanting wasn't good enough. Another lesson she'd learned too well. If something was going to happen, she had to make it happen. She couldn't rely on or trust anyone else.

"I really need to see him. If he's on the range, could you point me in his direction?" she asked.

Nancy looked stunned. "I— You've been away a long time, Kathryn. I don't know how much you knew of this place, but the Double Bar C is huge and pretty stark in places." Nancy glanced pointedly at Kathryn's car, down at her watermelon abdomen, then up at the sky. The day was sweltering, the sun relentless and blinding as a camera flash.

"I know, but I'll be fine. I'm a runner and these days I keep my phone handy," Kathryn said, ignoring her own misgivings. The ranch might have its stark areas, but the Calhouns had always run it like a well-oiled machine. Communication lines were kept open. "Or…I was a runner until recently. I'll be okay."

Nancy gave a curt nod. "Let me just call Holt." She paused. "I have to be honest. He's not going to like this."

"I know. Besides the fact that he's busy, I've

already called six times. If you're going to tell him anything, tell him that I'm—that I'm not giving up. I'll do whatever it takes. Including wandering all over the ranch looking for him."

That wasn't exactly true. She was trying to keep her courage up, to appear determined. Still, she wasn't stupid, and she didn't plan to wander far from the road. But for now, let Nancy—and Holt—think she was a crazy pregnant woman if that was the only way she could get his attention. Frustration and fear were making her a bit desperate. She needed to get as much done as possible before the baby arrived.

"All right. I'll see what I can do." Nancy retreated to the other end of the room, speaking into the phone quietly. She appeared to be holding her hand over the receiver, too, but even so, Kathryn could still hear Holt's curse when he realized what was happening.

"Just find out where he is." She gave Nancy an apologetic look. "I'll handle the rest. You shouldn't have to deal with my problems."

Instead, Nancy listened to whatever Holt was

saying, then directed Kathryn to a seat in the living room. "He's coming."

And he clearly wasn't happy about the situation. Kathryn could see it in the strain in Nancy's eyes.

"Do you mind if I sit on the porch? I'd rather face him head-on. Outdoors. Just in case he throws anything at me." She smiled slightly when she said it, trying to make it sound like a joke, but it wasn't completely. She'd lived her whole life with people who were prone to sudden outbursts of anger. It was always good to have an exit plan.

Nancy gave her a stern look. "Suit yourself, but Holt would never throw anything at a woman. Especially a pregnant one."

Kathryn nodded and marched to a rocking chair on the big low porch. She could tell by Nancy's look that the woman wondered about whatever circumstances had led to Kathryn being alone and pregnant, but she wasn't sharing that with anyone. Not Nancy. Certainly not Holt.

Not that the man would ask. He didn't even want to see her. She was surprised he even remembered who she was.

Maybe he doesn't, she thought. He'd always looked right past her when she was a skinny, lovesick teenager and he was a moody, broody football player who barely said a word to anyone and never even said hello to her.

She'd daydreamed about him being like her, kindred souls trapped in untenable circumstances with no one to confide in.

Of course, she'd been wrong. He'd simply been a guy who hadn't noticed or cared. And clearly nothing had changed with him.

A lot had changed with her. Except for the fact that she still got tense just thinking of Holt coming down the road, exiting his car and stepping onto the porch.

Which was totally nuts. She didn't have room or the inclination for a man in her world anymore. Especially not this man.

And anyway—a dust cloud in the distance heralded an oncoming vehicle—there was no time to do anything but brace herself. She and Holt were going to talk.

Finally.

Holt threw open the truck's door. He started

toward her, big and imposing with a granite jaw and dark eyes that told her she'd pushed him too far.

Kathryn swallowed hard. She reminded herself that she was a full-grown woman, almost ten years older than she'd been the last time she'd seen Holt. And determined to be what she hadn't been then. Strong. Independent. Not affected even by a man as overwhelming as Holt.

"Hello, Holt," she said, rising a bit more awkwardly than she wanted to and holding out her hand in as casual a gesture as she could muster. "Thank you for stopping by." *How stupid. This was his home. And she was acting like a queen expecting him to kiss her hand.*

"Not an issue. I was headed in, anyway," he said, putting her in her place. "Besides, this won't take long."

She blinked. "How do you know that?"

"I know it, because the answer is no," he said, those dark caramel eyes smoldering. "I know why you're here. I *don't* know what the mayor said that led you to believe that I get involved in causes, but she was wrong. I do only one thing and that's ranch. I'm sorry you wasted your time, but I believe it's best to be honest."

Kathryn sucked in a breath and hoped that her knees weren't shaking. "I believe that, too. And the truth is that I don't intend to stop being a pest. You'll have to hear me out."

"I already know what you want. There's no point in discussing the details."

"Whatever you've been told, it's clearly not everything. And I intend to follow you around until you listen to the whole story." It was all she could do to keep her voice from wobbling. Not just because Holt was so big, with such broad shoulders, but because he was so…male. The fact that he was also hostile… Kathryn fought to stay calm. To remain standing.

"Excuse me?" He frowned, those fierce dark eyes making her squirm inside. She wondered how many women had ever told Holt Calhoun no. Probably not many.

Probably none. The man looked like the definition of sex, all long legs, muscles and thick tousled, near-black hair. He looked like a man who knew how to do things. And not just ranching things. Things that involved getting naked with a woman.

Which was totally irrelevant...and terribly distracting. "I mean it," Kathryn said. She frowned back at him, even if she was mostly upset at herself. Her Holt-crush years were long gone. She was going to be a mom. She needed to get her off-track life on track and do right by her baby, not get derailed by stupid, hormonally driven thoughts about a man who didn't even want to talk to her and who reminded her of the bad places she'd been, not the good places she wanted to go.

"You plan to follow me around?" he finally said. "Lady, do you even know what you're saying?"

No. "Yes. Mayor Hollis highly recommended you."

Holt swore beneath his breath. "Johanna is sharp as they come, but she's dead wrong about this."

"I don't think so. And you can't make me leave. I'm...I'm persistent." Which was such a lie. She'd never persisted with anything. And her ex-husband had loved to taunt her with that humiliating fact. Which might, she admitted, be a big part of why she had to persist with this now.

"This is a ranch," Holt reminded her. "It's big and dirty. There are animals that can break your foot if they step the wrong way or break your body if they fall on you. You are a pregnant woman."

"Yes. I've noticed."

He gave her a you-don't-know-a-thing look. "No following."

"Just give me a few minutes."

He started to say no. She was sure of it, but she stuck out her hand and touched his arm. His blue chambray shirtsleeve was worn. His muscle was firm and warm beneath her palm. Kathryn didn't know what the heck she was doing. She felt reckless and stupid and awkward, as she always had around him, but…

"We've already wasted several minutes arguing. Wouldn't it be easier just to listen to me?"

"I have the feeling that nothing about this will be easy."

So did she. "Just a few minutes," she prompted.

"All right. Let's get this over with. Sit. Talk." He turned a chair backward, straddled it and looked at his watch. "You have ten minutes. No more."

Kathryn swallowed hard and tried to find the right words. For the first time in her life she had Holt Calhoun's attention and she couldn't afford to waste the opportunity. There was too much at stake.

Holt felt like a volcano, bubbling hot and on the verge of blowing up everything around him. What in hell had the mayor been thinking when she'd recommended that he be the one to help Kathryn Ellis? And what was this about, anyway? Some nonsense about a clinic and donors, whatever that meant.

He wanted this conversation to be over, but he'd promised her ten minutes. And just look at her. Despite being heavily pregnant, which brought back terrible memories he didn't even want to acknowledge, she was slender, bone-china fragile, and when she looked at him...

He noticed how her dark blond hair, streaked

with a hundred shades of wheat, kissed her delicate jaw, how those big gray eyes looked so anxious. Despite her determined words, this woman looked as if a sharp wind could break her, both physically and emotionally. And then there was the fact that she was pregnant. That made her the last person in the world a man like him should be around. He'd seen her from a distance in town after the mayor had mentioned the situation, so he'd already decided that this wasn't happening. And not just because he didn't want to do what he'd heard she wanted him to do.

"Ms. Ellis," he began.

"I'm Kathryn. You knew me when I was a teenager."

He'd known who she was. Vaguely. A skinny, scared-looking little creature. That's all he remembered. And by calling her by her last name he'd been trying to create distance, to make a point. "Ms. Ellis," he said determinedly. "I'm afraid you've been led astray."

"Johanna said you had business and political contacts that no one else in town has. Is that true?"

"It may be. But it's irrelevant."

"I'm sure you've heard why I'm here."

He knew what he'd heard. The town already had a clinic, so…

"Why don't you just spell it out?"

"I'm trying to get a new medical clinic built in Larkville. And lure a permanent doctor here. To do that, we may need the help of influential people."

"Johanna's the mayor. She has political contacts."

"She's the mayor of a town of less than two thousand. Her influence is limited. Your family name is known by people in high places."

"I don't suck up to them. I don't ask favors. Ever." He glared at her.

"I'm not asking you to—to prostitute yourself," she said, all prim and librarian-like. Her eyelashes drifted down, just a bit before she righted them. Her slender hands were in tight fists. She was clearly nervous. Because she was determined to drag a yes from him or because he was out-and-out scaring her?

Holt wanted to let loose with a string of blue

curses. He was rotten at situations like this, at dealing with women with expectations. He'd learned from his mother, his father, from his former fiancée, Lilith, that needing, caring, wanting too deeply, expecting too much, came with a hefty price tag. Emotion could cripple. He knew that. He'd paid that price before and was still paying it. So while he was used to doing all kinds of favors as the owner of the Double Bar C and he did them willingly, he kept things cut and dried, light, easy, uncomplicated by emotions. And he didn't ask for favors himself. He was pretty sure based on what he'd heard that Kathryn Ellis was asking him to break several of his unbreakable rules. *Be the giver, not the recipient. Remain in control of the situation at all times. Never let emotion enter into a deal.*

"You'll have to be more specific than that," he told her. "Just what are you asking me to do?"

"I want you to help me get the clinic off the ground. I want you to help me get funding."

"Which will most likely mean prostituting myself, as you put it."

"Not necessarily. Some people will give out of the goodness of their hearts."

"For a clinic that will only benefit one very small town."

"It's your hometown."

"It's not *their* hometown. You're talking about people who have a million life-or-death causes pounding on their doors every day."

Kathryn blinked. She bit her lip. "I suppose that's true, but...you're Holt Calhoun. You could convince them."

The way she said that made it sound as if he could do anything. And no one knew better than he did how wrong that was. Pain sliced through him like a razor. Easy. Devastating. He slapped the flat of his hand against the porch post. "Dammit. Lady, I may not know much about you, but you obviously don't know me at all."

She looked to the side as if he'd embarrassed her. Maybe he had. Tact wasn't his strong suit. And frankly, he didn't care.

"We need a doctor," she said. "I work part-time in Dr. Cooper's office. He's moving to California to be near his son, and then there'll be no one.

And the clinic, if you want to call a two-room building with an examination room the size of a closet a clinic, is crumbling."

"I've heard that it's slightly outdated." But only in passing when Wes, his foreman, had gone in for some minor treatment.

"It's more than outdated. It's inadequate, and once Dr. Cooper leaves, we're never going to be able to lure another doctor here to work in such a tumbledown facility."

"I see. But Austin is only forty miles away and there are doctors there."

She crossed her arms. It made her ample breasts more noticeable, and also emphasized her heavily rounded belly. She was a pretty woman, a delicate one, and her pregnancy only seemed to emphasize that delicate beauty. He could have slapped himself for noticing any of those things. "In an emergency, forty miles might as well be four hundred," she pointed out.

"I see, Ms. Ellis. You're concerned about the trip to the hospital." He did his best not to think of another situation, another pregnant woman. Anger, dark and reckless, filled his soul.

"Stop that," she said. "Stop pretending you don't know my name. And this isn't for me. I'm due to deliver in a matter of weeks. By the time the clinic is built...*if* it's built," she emphasized, turning those big, plaintive eyes on him, "I'll be long gone."

That got his attention. "Let me get this straight. You want to build a clinic in a town you don't even intend to live in. Why?"

"I have my reasons. They don't matter. They're not the point."

And she clearly wasn't going to share them. That was okay. A man like him who never shared his innermost thoughts couldn't blame someone else for holding back. Still, now that they'd slid past the topic of her pregnancy, he could deal with reality. He wasn't the answer to anyone's prayers and he never had been. Head down, he ran the ranch and he did it well. He did what was necessary. But he never strayed beyond that. He couldn't.

"I'm sorry," he said. And a part of him meant that most sincerely. "But it's not happening. I've been away from the ranch for too long." For reasons he wasn't prepared to discuss. "And despite the fact that I have a top-notch foreman and crew, there's a truckload of work to be done. I'm not who you need, and I don't have the time, the inclination or the ability to help you."

"Not even if we're talking life or death?" she asked, emphasizing that fact again. Something in her eyes told him that he'd disappointed her. Well, nothing new there. He was an excellent rancher, but he was also a master at disappointing people who expected him to care too much.

"You've been led astray if you were told to expect this kind of help from me," he said. "I confine myself to small favors, to the doable. I'm no miracle worker."

He stared coldly into her eyes, doing his best to ignore the fear and pain there, the slide of something—a tiny foot, a hand?—across her belly or how she automatically placed her palm over that place.

Her gray eyes pleaded with him, but she said nothing. A sudden, vague memory of a young girl looking at him as if she expected him to answer all her prayers flashed across his memory and was just as quickly gone.

His phone rang, and he deliberately put it on speakerphone. Anything to fill the silence. His foreman, Wes, said, "Holt, that cow with bloat needs seeing to or we're going to lose her. The vet's in the next county and you're the best one to handle something this complicated."

"I'll be there in five." Holt clicked off. He turned to Kathryn. "I have to go," he said. Not *I'm sorry,* or *Excuse me.* The sudden defeat in her eyes made him want to say those words, but that might have given her hope for something that just wasn't going to happen. He wasn't the savior she had hoped he would be, and he wouldn't pretend otherwise.

Her shoulders slumped. She turned toward her rusting car, then turned back. "Off to work a miracle, Holt?" she asked, throwing his "I'm no miracle worker" comment back at him.

"Off to do what I know how to do," he said. "I don't promise what I can't deliver. Ever."

And miracles of any kind were well outside his realm. As he had learned only too well.

Not waiting for her to leave, he strode to his truck. As he drove away in a cloud of dust, a pair of gray, hopeful eyes taunted him.

This time he didn't hold back. He let loose with a string of blue language. Ms. Kathryn Ellis didn't know how lucky she was. Women who got involved with an unbending, emotionally stingy man like him lived to regret it. As he'd been told before.

CHAPTER TWO

OKAY, dealing with Holt wasn't going to be simple, Kathryn thought, back at home. If there was anyone else… But the mayor was adamant that he was the only one in a town this size who had the kind of influence she needed. The Double Bar C was known nationwide. The Calhouns had their fingers in many pies, and Holt was the one who oversaw all of that.

None of that would mean a thing, though, if the man didn't agree to lend a hand. What to do? What to do? And why did it matter so much?

Because she was determined to turn her life completely around and this was the first step. *I came back to my parents' empty house despite the bad memories because I had no money or work,* Kathryn reminded herself. Most of her life had been like that, running from one bad situation and one place to another. But with a baby on the way, she had to do more, to take a stand and become the kind of person a child could depend on. The next time she left somewhere she was going to do it the right way, having left something good behind her, because there was something good ahead of her.

Helping to build this clinic offered her a chance to leave this place on a positive note. On a more major note, it would allow her to use her heretofore useless degree in urban planning and beef up her skimpy résumé. Overseeing the project was the kind of thing that might put a gleam in an employer's eye and finally help her provide a secure future for her and Baby Ellis.

But there was one more big reason. Despite her intent to slip quietly in and out of Larkville, she'd found that with her parents gone, the town was rather charming. She'd made a few friends, some of them her patients. She cared about them, worried about them and understood how scared they were at the prospect of losing their medical care. How could she not try to help? Still, even the best urban planner needed good people helping her. In this case, she had to get Holt's help. How?

Butter him up, she thought. *Flatter him. Play to his weaknesses.* Everyone had weaknesses, didn't they?

Kathryn splayed her hands across her belly as if communing with her child would help her focus her thoughts. "Play to Holt Calhoun's weaknesses?" As if she knew what those were.

Well, maybe she did, a little. During the two years she'd lived here, she'd practically stalked Holt. Other than football, he'd spent most of his time on the ranch. Cows, horses, dogs would be high on his list, she assumed. She hated having to brave the ranch again, but she had no choice. Where else would he be?

"You can do this, Ellis." Her words more bravado than fact. Still, she slipped on her maternity jeans, tennis shoes and a pink top and headed to the Double Bar C. When she arrived, she made a beeline for the stables. A bold move, because she was a little afraid of large animals. She might have lived in Texas, but her parents had been former city dwellers who hadn't liked Larkville. Ranches hadn't been part of her life. Too bad.

She was on a mission to rewrite the future, and it all started here. She wasn't running this time.

A snorting, snuffling sound came from her right where a white horse in the corral was tossing its head. It was a beautiful animal. A gigantic animal. And it didn't seem to be too sure about her presence.

Kathryn tried to quiet her nerves. She'd come prepared, knowing that Holt's animals would be a part of this. If she could make friends with this creature quickly, then when Holt finally showed up, he might think she was a natural cow woman, like her better, and he and she might bond over equine details. She had gone online just last night to find some interesting facts. She now knew that there were more than three hundred and fifty breeds of horses and ponies and she knew that horses could walk, trot, gallop and canter.

But none of that mattered right now. Holt's horse was looking at her as if she had horns and a red forked tail. Reaching for what she hoped would be her secret weapon, Kathryn dug into her purse and pulled a carrot from a plastic bag.

"Here, boy." She held out the carrot clutched

between her thumb and forefinger. "Look what I have."

The horse lurched toward her a bit, and she jerked back, then stuck her hand out again.

"Don't. Do. That." The deep voice was unmistakable. It came from the barn behind her. "Stop moving. Right now."

Kathryn froze. Holt walked up behind her, and she felt very exposed even though she was fully dressed. Seriously, the man exuded something masculine. He got attention.

But, of course, she was supposed to be the one snagging *his* attention, not the other way around.

"He doesn't like carrots?" she asked.

"He loves carrots."

"I—I see. Or, actually, I don't." She forgot to freeze and waved her hand around as she spoke. The horse followed with his head. He moved closer. Quickly.

Kathryn jumped.

Just then Holt stepped forward, gave a command to the horse and reached out and took her hand, forcing her to drop the carrot in the dirt. She looked at it with dismay.

"Why did you do that?"

"Because I assume you'd like to keep all your fingers. Horses have sharp teeth and massive heads. Daedalus is gentle, but he doesn't know you or understand what you're doing. He wants what you have, but the way you're bobbing around, he'll have to lunge for it, and his teeth might nip you. Or that big head of his might knock you on your rear." Holt shook his head as if he'd had to explain to a child not to cross the street without looking.

"I—" Kathryn felt herself blushing. "Thank you. I didn't realize. I didn't think, I guess."

"But you lived here in horse country." His words were clipped. He looked as if he thought she was lying.

"I only lived here two years, and we didn't have horses. My father came here following a job and he…well, he liked his privacy. He didn't like me making friends, so I didn't have any reason to learn about ranch life."

"And yet here you are trying to feed my animal."

She raised her chin. "Just because I didn't have

horses doesn't mean I don't want to know more about them. He's a spectacular horse. And this is a…it's a lovely ranch."

"I like it." He stared her down.

"I'd—I'd really like to know more about ranching."

"Just out of the blue like that? Planning to move to a ranch, are you?" He looked mildly amused. As if he was trying to keep from laughing.

Oh, no. Did he think she was flirting with him, pursuing him?

"No. I'm looking for a job in a city, but odds are my baby will be born here, and I want to be able to tell her a bit about her birthplace." As she said the words, Kathryn realized it was true. She *did* want her child to know something of her history. Because that kind of anchor had been missing from her own life. Her parents had moved constantly. They'd never discussed their lives before she'd been born. They'd never talked much at all without arguing or criticizing their only child for being a disappointment. Her ex-husband had continued the trend. Control by ignoring or criticizing her. Or making her feel that she was being unreasonable or demanding. It had been an effective system. Kathryn had always fallen into line. This time had to be different. She couldn't let Holt's opinion daunt her.

"So you want a history lesson and a tour. And you decided this when? This morning?"

She took a deep breath. "I—no—yes—no. I made that up about thirty seconds ago," she admitted, in part because Holt made her far too self-aware, but also because she just didn't want to get in the habit of lying. Good mothers didn't lie. And, oh, she really wanted to be a good mother.

Holt shook his head again. "If you want a history lesson or information on how a ranch runs, I'll point you in the direction of some books."

"I want more than that."

That had probably been the wrong thing to say. There was always the chance that he knew how big a crush she'd had on him when she was young. She hoped not, but the dark, fierce look in his eyes…the heat that rose within her…

Kathryn took a step backward. She caught her foot on something, a rock or… Suddenly she was slipping.

Just as suddenly, she wasn't. Holt's big hands were on her arms. He was pulling her upward, toward him. Her heart was thundering, her breath was erratic. And then she was free, standing on her own. Trying to act as if she was perfectly fine.

"I'm perfectly fine," she said.

A look of something that might have been amusement flitted across his face and then was gone. "Good. I was going to ask that in a minute." Even though he'd had no reason to ask. She hadn't even gotten near to hitting the ground. His quick reflexes and strong arms had seen to that. But his tone—was the darn man teasing her?

"I—I assumed as much," she said lamely, flustered, not happy that she was letting Holt get to her. But hadn't she always? Had she ever seriously thought they could be a couple when she was a starstruck teenager? She must have been insane. He was the worst kind of man for someone like her. Too intimidating, entirely too physical. His very presence made her feel as if her brain had gone missing. And her plan to butter him up, to humor him? The one that had seemed so right his morning?

It wasn't going to happen. He wasn't a man who craved adoration. If he had been, he would have scooped her up in high school and had all the adoration he could handle. She sighed.

"What?"

She forced herself to look straight into his eyes and not flinch. "I came here intending to schmooze you."

"I see. And how exactly were you going to do that?"

She looked at Daedalus. "Nice horse," she said weakly. "Nice hat."

He almost looked as if he wanted to smile.

Kathryn sighed again. "I'm afraid I'm not very good at schmoozing," she admitted. "I feel totally silly."

"Well, I've been told that I don't know how to accept a compliment, so..."

Yeah, it had been a bad, unworkable idea. "I should go." Kathryn realized that she was still standing far too close to Holt. His sheer size, the breadth of his shoulders, was forbidding. He was quite possibly the most masculine male she could ever remember meeting.

Not that it mattered. Even if she hadn't been extremely pregnant, she was never going to allow herself to think of a man that way again. Especially not a man like Holt. He was the type who could swallow her soul and mangle it, when she had barely escaped her mistake of a marriage with her soul intact. Still, with her retreat she felt her grand plans evaporating. Holt wasn't going to help her. She would have no project to her name, nothing to put on her résumé, probably no means of supporting herself and her child once the clinic closed. And her friends she wanted to help…that wasn't going to happen, either. She was going to fail at all of that. Just because of this stubborn man.

No, that wasn't right. It wasn't him. She was the one who had to convince him to help her. Winning others' cooperation would be a big part of her job if she ever managed to get a job in her field. This was her proving ground.

Kathryn forced herself to look straight into

Holt's eyes. "Don't you care about the people of the town?"

He didn't answer that, but his brows drew together in a scowl.

"I see them," she said. "Every day. People who come to Dr. Cooper with serious, frightening problems."

As if she'd said something offensive, his expression turned colder. Without thought, she shoved her hand out and blindly touched his shoulder. Instantly, his muscles flexed beneath the pads of her fingertips. Her hand tingled, her heart took an extra beat. Kathryn jerked back as if she'd touched fire.

The look in his dark eyes was deadly. "Don't make the mistake of thinking I'm going to discuss my feelings."

No, she could see that would be a mistake. "I won't, but—"

He raised one dark, sexy brow, and Kathryn had to work to stay focused. "But what do you think will happen if people don't have a clinic or a doctor in Larkville?" she continued.

"It's not something I've spent a lot of time thinking about."

"Of course not. You're clearly an incredibly healthy man."

He blinked, as if she'd said something shocking when all she'd said—did he think she was ogling him?

Most likely. Women would. *She* had in the past, and if her circumstances and her life and her entire world hadn't turned out the way it had… No, no, no.

"I only meant that you've obviously not spent a lot of time in doctors' offices," she said a bit too quickly.

He didn't respond.

"But there are people who need regular treatments or who need help quickly. If a doctor isn't nearby, they may put off going at all. They might even die. Think about that."

He frowned at her. "I'm thinking," he said. And clearly what he was thinking wasn't anything good. Why, oh, why was Holt the man she had to work with in order to get this thing done?

* * *

Holt felt as if he'd been kicked in the gut. By something a lot bigger and more lethal than this fragile woman standing before him. Kathryn wasn't just looking for a favor. He was used to doing small favors. Like it or not, they were part of the ranch's role in the community. But Kathryn wanted more than a small favor. She wanted *him* to ask for favors, and that wasn't his style. The thought of opening himself up that way, begging, burned him like fire. What's more, for a minute he had thought she'd wanted him to discuss his feelings. And he definitely wasn't that guy. He worked, he did his duty, but discussing what he felt—or did not feel—was for other men. Actually, indulging in those deeper emotions was for other men, too.

Still, he looked down into those pretty eyes and realized he could no longer ignore her request for a favor. His father, Clay, had died of pneumonia when he'd refused to see a doctor until it was too late. And his friend and former ranch hand, the one he'd been with these past few months… what if Hank had gone to the doctor and found his cancer sooner?

Holt swore beneath his breath.

Kathryn wrapped her arms around her abdomen as if those slender arms could protect the child inside. That single movement made him remember things, feel raw inside. He didn't like that one bit.

But as if his swearing had unleashed something in her, she changed before his eyes. "Okay, I get it. You're never going to help." Her eyes flashed fire, and suddenly she didn't look so fragile anymore. She looked a bit like a miffed tigress. "I hate to say this, Holt, but sometimes I don't like men very much." With an accusing look, she swung her head and turned to go, her blond hair catching on the pale pink collar of her blouse, exposing her long, slender neck. And whether it was her tigress ways or that beautiful neck, a jolt of physical awareness shot through him.

Don't notice that, he told himself, trying to ignore the instant heat that her innocent manner and her movement had called forth in him. *Don't think of her that way.* Kathryn was a woman on a mission, a woman dedicated to passionate causes, and a woman with a baby on the way. She wasn't in the market for anything short-lived or based on physical chemistry alone, while he wasn't open to anything more. He didn't get involved with women who wanted too much from him. After Lilith, he especially didn't get involved with pregnant women. The fact that Kathryn was both passionate and pregnant made her radioactive. A woman to steer *around,* not get close to.

And yet, here he was, thinking about the long, naked column of her neck and trying not to think about any more of her naked. Holt wanted to swear again. He held back.

At that moment, Blue, Holt's German shepherd mix, wandered near. Blue was big and slobbery with a torn ear. He looked like a dog who could eat humans just for fun, and most people kept their distance when they first met him.

Kathryn bent over and held her hand out to him so he could sniff and make up his mind about her, then rubbed him behind his ears just as if he was a cute little puppy. Blue looked as if he was in ecstasy.

"He's a killer," Holt said, disgusted with Blue, but mostly with himself.

"I can see that. You trained him to go for the throat?"

Holt raised one brow. "I trained him for a lot of things. Right now he seems to have forgotten all of them. I guess you're better at schmoozing than you thought."

She glanced up quickly and evidently noticed him staring at her. A delicious pale pink climbed her throat, making him want to groan.

Kathryn quickly looked at Blue. "No, he just likes to be rubbed."

"Who doesn't?" Had he really said that? Oh, yeah, he had. The startled look in her eyes left no question. The woman was shocked. Just yesterday he would have been glad. But today she had made him think about things he couldn't ignore. He was going to say yes. The truth was that he couldn't have anyone else on his conscience. He already had a whole lot to answer for, things he struggled not to think about every day, and like it or not, he was going to have to get mixed up in Kathryn's passionate project and do a bunch of things he didn't like.

But two things he wouldn't do. He wouldn't

expose his soul, his demons, that part of himself only he was privy to, by letting her know just how she'd talked him into this. And he wouldn't let her be in control the way it had gone down with Lilith.

Time to do a little creative backpedaling. Somehow.

"I probably shouldn't have made that last comment about Blue," he began, not very smoothly.

At his name, Blue's ears perked up a bit, but he was still looking like some lovesick fool, slobbering all over Kathryn's hand. What was it with the woman?

"So you think I should help you get this clinic built?" he asked, stalling while he tried to think of some good idea. She was looking at him as if he'd been the one who'd slipped and maybe hit his head on a rock. And why not? The woman had been all but begging him to help her for days.

"I do. I really do."

"How do I know you're not just some Goody Two-shoes who gets fired up about causes and then drops them to move on to the next one? You just said that you weren't staying."

"I'm not. I'm an urban planner. The jobs I'm looking for will be in cities and I have a baby to support, but I assure you that I won't run out on this project."

"How do I know that you're truly dedicated?"

She raised that pretty chin. "You could try taking my word on it."

He shook his head slowly, almost sadly. "Kathryn, Kathryn, I'm a businessman. I can't just take your word on things." Even though he did that every day. But she couldn't know that. And anyway, he didn't really know her. There was a good chance she might bolt and he would be left with a mess on his hands.

"And this project will take time away from my ranching duties. I might have to set a few things aside. Like…"

He paused.

"Like…" she prompted.

"Well, like Blue here. He's used to me having time to put him through his paces. What if I don't have time for that stuff?"

She raised one pretty brow. "You're telling me that the only thing holding you back is that you're worried you won't have time to exercise Blue?"

The dog moaned when she said his name as if he'd been waiting for her to do that all his life.

Holt gave him the evil eye. Which Blue ignored.

"A man's dog is his best friend."

"You have friends, then?" she asked, still in full tigress mode.

Holt looked taken aback. "That seems like a snotty thing to say to a man when you've asked him to do you a favor."

She blushed that pretty pink that started somewhere beneath her clothing, and Holt swallowed hard. "You're right. Of course," she agreed. "What if—if you get bogged down and can't take care of Blue, I could, er, put him through his paces?"

"And you think it's my duty to the town to take care of getting this clinic?"

"Just to help. I'll be doing a lot of it, too."

"Ah."

"Are you trying to intimidate me?"

He shrugged. "Is it working?"

"No."

"Good. Because I was really just testing you to

see how dedicated you are. So you'll do a lot of the work, you'll walk my dog and you'll—what?"

Kathryn raised herself up to her full height. Despite being shorter than him and very pregnant, she somehow managed to look down her nose at him. "I'll make sure that your town has a first-rate clinic, Mr. Calhoun."

He nodded, then turned to the dog. "What do you think, Blue?"

The dog turned sad eyes on Kathryn and nudged closer, obviously hoping for more of that rubbing. Then to Holt's surprise, Blue gave a little woof. That wasn't like him. He was well trained, and he didn't bark unless there was a reason to bark.

Kathryn crossed her arms. "I suppose you're going to tell me that Blue doesn't think the clinic is a good idea."

Holt wanted to smile, but he managed to refrain. Kathryn Ellis was pretty cute when she was miffed. Why had he never noticed that before?

"Not at all. Blue thinks I should sleep on what you've said and then I'll give you my reply tomorrow." If they were going to work together, he was going to call the shots. He wasn't going to risk a repeat of Lilith.

"I see."

She didn't, of course, but he had to give her credit for being a good sport about the whole thing.

"This isn't a joke," she said quietly.

She was right. "No, ma'am, it isn't. I'll be in touch. Real soon. That's a promise." And for some reason he couldn't fathom, he held out his hand. It was, possibly, the dumbest thing he'd done in a long time.

Kathryn placed her hand in his and he closed his big palm around her much smaller one. As her skin slid against his, he was more aware of her as a woman than he'd been when he was undressing other women.

Quickly, she pulled away. Good idea.

Not like this business of him and Kathryn working together, he thought after she'd gone. That had *bad idea* written all over it. Unfortunately, he was already in. Now all he had to do was tell her. For real this time. Maybe he'd be lucky and she would decide he was a crazy man and find someone else to ask her favors for her.

But he knew that that was a long shot. Kathryn was determined to get her clinic, even if she had to put up with a man like him to get it.

Still, he bet it would be a long time before she would let him shake her hand again. That was a shame. And a blessing. At least one of them was thinking straight. It sure wasn't him. Or Blue.

A short time later his phone rang. It was his sister Jess. His other sister Meg and his brother, Nate, would probably have been in on the call, too, but Meg was living in California now and Nate was still overseas with the army.

"I heard that Kathryn Ellis went out to the ranch today," Jess said. "What did she want?"

He hesitated. "Mostly I think she just wanted to pet my dog."

"I doubt that," Jess said, laughing. "Secretive as ever, Holt? Are you going to help her with that clinic?"

"Haven't decided yet."

"Did she give you her reasons for wanting to build it?"

Oh, no, he wasn't going there. Jess didn't know exactly how much their father had suffered or about the nightmares that kept him awake at night about their father's last days. She certainly didn't know the horrors that his friend Hank had faced and she knew nothing at all of what had gone on between himself and Lilith. "We discussed a few things," he said.

Jess sighed loudly. "You are the most frustrating man. Some day someone is going to get you to open up and talk."

"I talk." They saw each other frequently. But he also kept things to himself, kept things from the rest of the family, as he always had. That was his duty and right as the eldest. He knew that, just as he knew that Kathryn Ellis was not a part of his destiny.

That didn't mean he could keep her waiting forever. By tomorrow she would be pacing the floor and she wouldn't care two hoots about why he was going to help her. She'd just be glad that he was finally saying yes. He hoped.

CHAPTER THREE

THE next day after work Kathryn returned to her house with the almost-peeled-away white paint and the tilting porch where some of the boards were rotted through. Her parents hadn't been able to find a buyer for the house when they divorced so it had sat here neglected and forgotten. She supposed she should be grateful that neither of them was interested enough to object to her staying here. Otherwise, she'd be out on the streets.

She freelanced at the local newspaper and did odd jobs around the clinic a few afternoons a week, but this afternoon she had nothing. The inactivity unnerved her. Not having a full-time job or any solid plan for the future scared her to death, so after lunch she tried to dredge up a positive outlook, donning her I'm-planning-for-the-future attitude. She sent off a few résumés the way she did every day even though she hadn't gotten any nibbles.

Still, she was determined to move forward. So after lunch, she moved out onto the rickety porch swing with a pen and paper and began work on her doctor/clinic list. She tried not to think about the fact that Holt had promised her an answer today and that the answer might be no. She also tried not to remember how it had felt when he'd held her hand. Sensation had ping-ponged through her body. And it had been much hotter than anything she'd felt in high school.

"The man is impossible," she muttered. He could have given her his answer yesterday. That made her think that the answer was going to be no and he was just trying to come up with a way to let her down easy. This was almost like a repeat of high school, with her wanting something from him she couldn't have. The only difference was that this time she didn't daydream about him bending her back over the hood of his car and kissing her with wild abandon.

I don't, she insisted as a hot sizzle went through her. "Because that would be completely inappropriate for an about-to-burst pregnant woman." Not to mention stupid and totally disastrous for someone like herself. She'd learned a lot of lessons during these past few years of being married to a man who was controlling, judgmental and inclined to bursts of cruelty, but the most important went something like this. *Don't get too close to imposing, hard-to-deal-with men like Holt.* James was a larger-than-life, brooding type just like Holt. People admired him and told her that still waters ran deep, but what she'd found was that behind that tough, quiet facade was a man with no soul and a lot of pent-up anger. Faced with that kind of man again, she knew to run. A woman who had been naive enough to fall for a man who hurt her would have to be ten kinds of stupid and something not very admirable if she did it again. But she wouldn't let that happen.

Maybe she could do the entire project herself.

A groan escaped her and she closed her eyes at the impossibility of it all. These kinds of opportunities didn't drop in everyone's lap. This was her ticket to security for her unborn baby, herself and the people of the town who needed good medical care—yet she was already flailing because, once again, she couldn't win over Holt Calhoun.

The sound of boots on pavement made her open her eyes.

As if her thoughts had conjured him up, Holt was crossing the street, heading toward her house. Dressed in jeans slung low on his hips and a pristine white shirt open at the throat, he was like some bronzed cowboy god with that dark hair and chiseled jaw. Instantly and against her will, her body reacted. When his gaze met hers, Holt nodded hello. Without waiting for her to invite him onto the porch, he simply stepped up as if he was used to doing what he wanted and going where he wanted. He probably was.

She struggled to stand so that she would be at less of a disadvantage. Unfortunately, her unwieldy body defied her.

Holt held out a hand as if to stop her. "No need. I just came to tell you not—"

"Holt? Is that you?" A woman's voice had them both looking toward the road. Kathryn peered around Holt to see Mrs. Best, a retired schoolteacher and one of Dr. Cooper's regular patients staring up at Holt as if she adored him. "It *is* you." She sounded delighted. "I haven't seen you since you came home, but I've been meaning to call."

"Good morning, Mrs. Best." Holt's voice was utterly polite, but after his atypical teasing bout with Blue yesterday he had retreated back to strong, silent cowboy mode.

"How nice to see two of my former students together in one place," the woman said. "I don't often, you know. Kathryn was from my last class just before I retired. I remember you had such a crush on Holt back then. It was so cute."

Kathryn wanted to find a place to hide, a tall order at this stage of her pregnancy. She felt her face heating up. "I was very young," she said. She wanted to add the words *and stupid,* but it probably wouldn't do to antagonize Holt when he hadn't given her an answer yet. After all, her goal was to build a clinic, not marry the man. And— fingers crossed—if he said yes, maybe the time spent together would clear away the last skeletal vestiges of his attraction for her. Because she now saw that he was a lot like James. Maybe she'd even been attracted to James because of her left-over crush on Holt. Sweeping him from her soul would be freeing. "I'm not a teenager anymore," she told both Mrs. Best and Holt. "Not so naive."

"Well. Things do change, don't they?" Mrs. Best asked, apparently realizing that she'd committed a faux pas. "It's good that you've grown up. If you hadn't, becoming a mama would probably have done the trick. It's a real responsibility. As a teacher, I saw my share of bad parents. Don't you be one."

If Kathryn hadn't been so scared of messing up as a mother, she might have smiled. Mrs. Best clearly hadn't given up teaching when she retired. Fortunately, she turned away from Kathryn and focused on Holt.

"Holt, I really did need to speak to you," she said. "I hate to mention this, but my fence that Clay built got damaged in the storm and if it's not fixed just right Bitsy gets out. While you were gone, I asked that idiot handyman, Donald, to take care of it, and the next thing you know, my little dog was chasing cars in the road. I've had to keep her in the house since then. I should have known not to trust it to anyone but you." She looked up at Holt as if she expected him to not only do something about her fence, but to restore world peace.

Holt only hesitated half a second. "I'll take care of it, Mrs. Best."

With a smile, the woman turned to go. "He's so good to all of us," she told Kathryn. "Just like his father." For a second she looked as if she might pat him on the cheek. Maybe Holt thought so, too. He had a wary look in his eyes.

Kathryn managed to contain her skepticism. When Mrs. Best walked away, she raised her chin. "So you're not as immune to requests as you seem."

"Fixing a fence is easy."

Maybe. Kathryn wasn't sure it would be easy for everyone. "What did she mean when she said that you're good to everyone?"

He frowned and shook his head. "Not important. Long story."

And one he clearly wasn't going to share with her. The man was certainly living up to that cowboy reputation as a rugged man of few words. It was such a cliché that she almost wanted to laugh.

Almost. Not quite. Holt *was* rugged, and staring up at him from her perch on the chair, she had to look up the entire length of his long, lean body. Pregnant as she was, she was still a woman, and despite her mistakes as a teenager and in her marriage, apparently not immune to Holt's physical charms. She pushed herself to her feet to break the spell and change the view to something less dangerous.

"But you *do* still consider requests for help," she prodded softly. She tried not to hope too hard.

"Depends on the request. Mrs. Best's is something I can do myself. Yours involved begging my friends for favors. I don't beg well. I don't ask for things. Even so, I came to tell you yes."

She blinked. She'd been prepared to argue more, even to plead a little.

"Just like that."

"No. Not just like that. I still don't like this any better than I did, but I'll do it."

"Why?"

"Don't push it, Kathryn. If you've decided you don't need my help after all, I'm better than fine with that."

"No. I want your help. I'll take it. You can't back out now."

His eyes narrowed. "I don't back out. Ever. Once I've given my word, it's golden. Understand?" The look he gave her might have killed a man. But she'd faced worse.

"Do you look at Blue like that?"

He looked taken aback. Then he gave her that maddening, half-amused expression. "Blue and I understand each other. Without speaking."

"My apologies. I'm not a wonderful and psychic dog but a decidedly human woman."

"Yes, I noticed. That you're not psychic. And that you're a woman."

He wasn't really even looking at her body. His gaze didn't drop, but she felt as if he could see through her clothing. Kathryn felt hot. And bothered.

"Okay," she rushed on, irritated that she couldn't seem to control her reaction to Holt. "I'll draw up some plans, all the things we need to do, and

I'll give you a copy so that you know your part and I know mine."

"Why are you doing that?"

She looked up, blinking wide. "I like organization. I make lists."

"No. You're rubbing your back. You're—you're real pregnant."

"Yes. I noticed."

He didn't smile at her sarcastic tone. "You should sit down. You don't need to stand."

Now he was making her mad. "Mr. Calhoun, I don't care to go into the details, but know this. I have been ordered around all my life and I'm done with that. I've thoroughly researched pregnancy, and Dr. Cooper and I have talked. I'm a healthy woman, and I'll let you know if I need to sit down."

He raised that sexy eyebrow that had always driven her mad. "I wasn't giving you an order." His voice was low and somewhat mocking.

"I— Yes," she stammered. "I understand that. My apologies for jumping to conclusions. Of course, you were just being polite."

He didn't answer her. But she didn't sit, either,

even though right now her legs were beginning to feel as if they wouldn't hold her up any longer. Her back *was* aching, and if Holt hadn't been here, she would have sat down, but the man had always made her feel weak. She had a bad feeling about what might happen if he knew that she was susceptible to him. It was very important that they keep things on a business footing during the remainder of her time in Larkville.

"Thank you for agreeing to help."

"I won't be available a lot of the time," he warned her. "Now that I'm back at the ranch, I have duties."

"We can meet there."

"I don't think we need to meet."

And she certainly didn't want to meet any more than was necessary, but…

"Humor a pregnant woman," she said, knowing that wasn't fair.

"Just send me a list. I'll do my part. And decide which parts I won't do."

With that, he walked away. For a few seconds, Kathryn wondered what she'd ever seen in him.

Other than that gorgeous body that could still

make her squirm. When she woke in the middle of the night having the "Holt dream," the one where he picked her up and carried her to his bed, the one where he came to her wearing nothing but an unzipped pair of jeans, the one where she finally got the chance to plunge her fingers into all that wonderful black hair, Kathryn knew she was going to have to be incredibly careful during her time here.

A man like Holt who could make a bloated, nearly-nine-months-pregnant woman feel desire was far too hot to handle. Good thing he didn't have a romantic bone in his body.

CHAPTER FOUR

THE first place Holt went the next morning was to the hangar on the ranch where he kept his Cessna and his helicopter. There was really no reason to do this. Both were kept in pristine condition, and he wasn't going anywhere. He didn't have any cows to herd out of remote locations. And he had no emergencies to tend to.

While he'd been away, his ranch hands had done their best to keep the place going, but the Double Bar C was big. He had plenty of tasks stacked up. Good. He needed some sweaty, back-breaking ranch work to clear his head and keep away any distracting thoughts of Kathryn. What was it about the woman that made her so tough to ignore? Was it the combination of delicate woman combined with that tigress determination? Or the fact that he could tell that he intimidated her but she still held her own with him?

He swore. Did it even matter? No, it didn't. Because he didn't want it to. They were going to have the equivalent of a "ten-minute business relationship." They were fire and ice, not a good combination. Plus, ranching was all he cared about, all he knew. It was what he was good at, and he wasn't good at relationships. At all. Not that it mattered.

Don't lose track of what's important, he could hear his father saying. *You're in charge of the Double Bar C, the family's legacy. When you're away from the ranch, remember who you are. You represent the biggest concern in the area, and people will look up to you. You have a responsibility to the ranch, and through the ranch a responsibility to the family and the town. The ranch is the one thing that will never fail you. Don't let anything interfere with that. Don't get sidetracked or weak and make foolish mistakes with a woman the way I once did, son. Wanting a woman too much can kill a man.*

Holt knew that his father had been talking about someone other than his mother—possibly his first wife—because he saw how his mother suffered for loving his father too much. Sometimes she cried; he remembered her telling him how his father had never really loved her and now he, her son, was becoming another cold, closed-off Calhoun male. She clung to him when Clay was away. He felt sorry for her, but her unhappiness only reinforced what his father had said. Giving in to emotion was a mistake.

That wasn't happening. He'd already made some pretty foolish mistakes. He'd already run into his own weaknesses, and he wasn't doing it again. He'd lost too much. But he didn't want to think about that now.

With a growl, he headed out. Riding across the land, he breathed in the scent of new-mown hay. This was his world, where he could forget his mistakes and just be himself.

So, he buried himself in work, and for the first time in weeks he felt good. Riding up to the house at the end of the day, he knew once again that he was where he needed to be. Just him, a few men, the animals and the land. That was all he wanted.

But when he opened the door, Nancy was waiting. "Kathryn Ellis called three times. I finally gave up and gave her your email address. You might want to check it. She seemed to think there were things you needed to know."

Instantly a vision of soft gray eyes came to him. Pink lips. Luscious breasts.

He fought that image. He reminded himself of the reasons he had to ignore those eyes and lips and breasts. Instead, he marched to his computer and downloaded her message, and the list she'd sent him. And the revised, longer list she'd sent. And two more lists: her part, his part, a timeline. Everything was color-coded. There were links to articles on communities that had built clinics, links to suggested fundraisers.

When he was done reading, Holt had to blink, he'd been staring at the screen so long. He was tired. He was also glad. Kathryn might be pretty and soft, and he might feel the urge to touch her whenever she was near, but she was a finicky list maker.

Good. That made her easier to ignore.

He didn't bother answering. He had his own way of doing things, and he'd already decided what he would and wouldn't do. One thing he wasn't going to do was follow his blasted instincts and kiss Kathryn's pretty pink lips. The irritating woman was clearly emotional about all this stuff, but he wasn't an emotional man. Never had been. Never would be.

And that was final.

Kathryn paced the floor of her house. She checked her email, which meant that she checked nothing. There were no messages from employers and no response from Holt.

For an entire week, she had called. She'd sent emails. She'd even mailed him a letter, just to be safe. Nancy had been unfailingly polite, but she was clearly a "Holt woman," loyal to her boss. She didn't want to discuss him, and Kathryn understood that. She wouldn't have discussed Dr. Cooper if someone had been trying to glean information on him.

But enough was enough. The clock was ticking—on two fronts. Baby Ellis had been kicking more and more. Her stomach felt like a giant exercise ball with the exercise taking place on the inside. And several of Dr. Cooper's patients were getting really worried.

"I know it's immature of me, Kathryn," Ava DuShay had said yesterday. "But sometimes when I think of Dr. Cooper leaving, I just see myself running after his car yelling, 'Please don't leave. I'm scared.' Because, you know, I'm old. I don't drive anymore. Getting to an Austin doctor would be near impossible."

Kathryn had tried to soothe Ava, but it was difficult when she understood. And it was infuriating that Holt had told her he would help and now he wasn't helping.

With a sigh of resignation, Kathryn grabbed some papers from her desk, went outside and got in her car. She didn't like getting too far from town anymore. A part of her was half-afraid that her less than dependable car would conk out on a lonely road and she would go into labor with no one around to help.

Still, with two weeks to go, she was probably safe, and she and Holt were at an impasse. He probably thought she would just disappear if he ignored her.

"Think again, ranch boy," she muttered as she drove to the Double Bar C.

She wasn't going to stop at the house, not without making a cursory attempt to find Holt on her own first. It wasn't fair to keep putting Nancy on the defensive, and besides, chances were good that if Nancy called Holt, he would simply give her some placating message and suggest Kathryn go home.

Nervous as she was, with a history of being easily cowed, Kathryn knew she was just going to have to suck it up and do the right thing. If she wanted to be a successful urban developer and a good example for her child, she needed to learn how to deal with adversity and difficult people. Holt was probably an excellent proving ground. But if she'd had a choice, she wouldn't have chosen to practice her negotiating skills on a man who had fueled her fantasies.

Driving over the road on Holt's land, Kathryn felt like a trespasser, but then she heard the sound of men shouting.

"Jackpot," she muttered. She wasn't far from the house. The building was just over the rise, but she wasn't sure her rattletrap vehicle could negotiate the uneven terrain where the voices were coming from without losing some vital parts, so she left her car and began to walk.

Soon she saw a series of pens, some sort of metal contraption and a group of men. There was a lot of swearing and good-natured joking going on. It blended with the bawling sound of animals, and as Kathryn grew closer, she saw that these were calves. Even a greenhorn like her could figure that out. She also saw that Holt, whose height and bearing made him stand out from the crowd, was in the thick of things.

Men were herding animals from one pen to another, into a narrow area of fencing and then into the metal contraption where the calf was caught in place. Then Holt took what looked like a syringe and gave the animal a shot in its shoulder, after which they let the animal out of the contraption and moved it out of the way so the next one could be brought in. It was fascinating, even though Kathryn didn't understand the whys and wherefores. What she understood was that if she waited long enough, Holt would finish and then she could swoop in on him.

She moved closer, intending to stay out of view, but the land was open here, and one of the men saw her. "Holt," he said. "Company incoming."

Holt stopped what he was doing. He glared at Kathryn. She was a good thirty yards from the chute where the men were gathered, but with those long legs of his, he crossed the distance and was standing next to her in a matter of seconds.

"I'm assuming you have a good explanation for why you're standing out in an open field under the blazing sun risking heatstroke and…"

He glanced down at her stomach.

She placed a palm over it as if her puny hand could hide her from his gaze. "I'm in no danger and neither is my baby," she said. "If I went into labor, I'm pretty sure that most of you know something about giving birth."

He looked horrified. She felt a bit horrified herself. It was totally unlike her to say something like that. "Not that I intend to give birth anytime today or anywhere near you."

"That's good to know. But you still haven't

given me an explanation of why you're near a big gathering of hoofed animals."

She looked around and saw that in addition to several pickup trucks and four-wheelers, there were a few horses. And, of course, all those calves.

"They're penned."

"Not the horses. And even with the calves, escapes have happened."

"They're…they're babies," she tried to argue.

"Big enough to run you over and trample someone your size if you got in their way. Big enough to hurt you and your baby."

"You're trying to scare me."

"I'm trying to get you to go home."

"I wouldn't be here if you'd answered any of my messages."

"They didn't need answering. I saw your list of what you wanted me to do. I'm doing what I thought needed doing."

"Which isn't all of it if you're saying it that way. And you haven't even told me what you've done. How can we be partners if you don't talk to me?"

He froze. "I'm not good at partnering with people. I like to work alone."

Which was a blatant lie. She pointedly looked toward the men, the ones he'd been working with only moments ago. He shrugged, not even remotely apologetic. "They don't send me fancy color-coded lists like you do, hon."

Kathryn blushed. She was pretty sure he had used that term in order to get the city girl to march back to town in a huff. But the way he said it... she instantly imagined him in a bed half-naked, his arms around a woman after they'd just—

Oh, no, she was *not* going to think of Holt naked. "I don't mind being called 'hon,'" she said, taking his dare.

To her surprise a brief smile flitted across his face. "Good to know. What else don't you mind?"

Okay, so he was better at the sexual dare game than she was, Kathryn conceded, knowing she was blushing. "I'll tell you what I like. I like organization. And clarity. That's why I make lists."

He gave a quick nod. "Fair enough. But I'm not a list maker. I'm a doer."

"You think I'm all talk and no action?" She

stared at him pointedly. He stared right back. There it was again, that sudden heat, and the sun had nothing to do with it. Her comment about action felt as if it had sexual undertones, as if she was back to the dares when she was clearly way in over her head with a man as physical as Holt. "I just want to make this happen," she said softly. "I think I've explained why."

"You're afraid that people will die." His voice was emotionless but, for half a second, she saw something in his eyes that looked like…intense pain. When she had told Johanna that Holt had agreed to help her, the mayor had seemed relieved. She'd told Kathryn that Holt had lost his father and a good friend within a short span of time and that he had been with the friend when he died.

"Maybe no one will," she said, not wanting to dredge up bad memories. "But it's still important." She told him about Ava, who couldn't drive to Austin, and he nodded. He knew Ava. No surprise. Didn't Holt know everyone?

He blew out a breath and looked to the side. "I've put a few things in motion. I'm working.

Just don't push too hard, Kathryn. I'm not malleable."

If he hadn't looked so frustrated, she might have laughed. Saying Holt wasn't malleable was like saying that grass wasn't purple. "What things?" she asked.

But at that moment, there was a lot of bawling. And yelling. Holt turned around and looked. So did Kathryn. Cowboys were swinging their hats. A calf had managed to get a good kick in. "I'll be in touch," he said.

Oh, no, he was dismissing her. Obviously he had to go. But she might never get near him again. She had to do something. "Wait!"

He turned back to her. And did as she asked. He waited.

"Are you okay?" He looked down at her stomach.

"I'm up here," Kathryn said. "And I'm fine." The man seemed very uncomfortable around her stomach, but she was so much more than a pregnant woman. At least she hoped so.

The bellowing in the background had faded

and things were proceeding. "What exactly are you doing here today?" she asked.

"We're vaccinating calves."

"They don't seem to like it."

"It's not their favorite thing, but then cows generally put eating at the top of their favorite things list. Everything else pales in comparison."

"They're cute," she decided, seeing one trying to lick a butterfly off its nose.

Holt looped his thumbs in his belt loops and looked down at the ground, as if praying for patience. Kathryn realized that she was doing this all wrong. She was probably alienating Holt, not winning him to her side. But the darn man made it hard to think straight when he stood there looking so, so Holt-ish.

She probably should leave. Right now. But she didn't.

CHAPTER FIVE

"Excuse me for a minute," Holt told Kathryn. He waved his hat and Dave, one of his men, came running. Holt stepped aside and talked to Dave, who nodded and walked away. In just a few minutes Dave returned with an old black canvas director's chair and a ragged umbrella he had fished out of someone's truck.

Holt unfolded the chair and held out his hand to Kathryn. "I'd feel a lot more comfortable if you sat down," he said. "And got out of the sun."

She nodded. "If it will make you feel better and loosen your tongue."

"It might." It wouldn't. He had never been much of a talker. It was one of his prime flaws, according to the women he had dated. It was definitely one of several reasons everything had gone so horribly wrong with Lilith and why he would never be a father. But he couldn't think about that.

Kathryn sat.

"Don't make the mistake of thinking these are puppies," he said. "One of these calves could drag you if you tried to lead him. Besides, they're not all that cute." Which was a lie. Some of them were very cute. But he didn't want her going all maternal on his animals and getting too close. Every cowboy had taken a few kicks. A pregnant woman couldn't risk even one.

"*I* think they're cute," she insisted. "And that contraption..." She frowned.

"It's a squeeze chute. We herd the calves through the pens, into the working chute and into the squeeze chute where they're held immobile to keep everyone, including the calf, safe while we give the injection."

"It looks like a torture device." She really was a city girl.

He nearly smiled. "Actually, the calves find being held tight, but not too tight, comforting. If they have room to buck, they work themselves into a frenzy. The chute prevents that. And the injection is given subcutaneously, so it's not in the muscle and is as painless as possible."

"Interesting."

He gave her a look of disbelief.

"No, I mean it. This is all new to me. I'll have stories to tell my child."

Stories. It reminded him of how Lilith, another city woman who had dropped into his life and dropped out again, had told him she'd once envisioned him as a romantic cowboy—but then he had disappointed her beyond belief.

He looked down at Kathryn. In her pale blue dress, she looked ethereal. With that wheat hair and those delicate arms curved around her stomach, she had *angel* written all over her.

The warnings that had been shooting through his brain ever since he'd first heard that Kathryn wanted his help intensified. He wasn't made to commune with angels. Especially since earthbound women had told him that he was the devil.

He leaned forward, placing his palms on the slender arms of the chair, moving into her space.

"This isn't a book, Kathryn. I'm not some romantic caricature of a cowboy. This is my life. It's not yours. So what are you doing here?"

She closed her eyes. One second went by. Two.

Then two more. This close to her, he was able to study her pale skin, her pink lips, her long eye-lashes drifting down over her cheeks. He had no business noticing any of that.

Suddenly she opened her eyes and he nearly sucked in his breath. There was too much feel-ing shining from the depths of those eyes. That couldn't be good.

"I'm here in Larkville because bad things hap-pened and I ended my marriage, I had no work, I'm having a baby and I had nowhere to go. Until I find a job as an urban developer, I work three days at the clinic and moonlight at the newspa-per. As for the rest, I'm not playing games, Holt. I've already explained to you how important this new clinic is. The town needs this, and I need the experience to help me win a position or else I'm going to end up destitute with no way to care for my baby. And yes, I really need your help, but I also need to be the driving force. So I made a plan and I make lists and apparently I'm making a nuisance out of myself."

Her voice was low. There was passion in her

eyes. He wanted to move closer. Much closer, and that would be a mistake.

He forced himself away from her. "Why do you need to be the driving force?"

She looked up at him. "I've been controlled by people all my life. Now I'm having a baby, and I can't be that weak person who just gives in anymore. Besides, if I'm going to prove I deserve the kind of job I want, I have to be a commanding force.

"As for me being romantic, yes, I *did* have a crush on you in high school, but so did every girl. Besides, that girl I used to be is gone. I've already done the romance and marriage thing and it was a mistake I don't want to repeat. Don't worry."

"I'm not worried. But I meant what I said. I'm not good partner material. Of any kind. Not romantic. Not otherwise. I have good employees here at the ranch, but there's a hierarchy."

"There won't be a hierarchy with us."

He crossed his arms.

She placed her hands on the chair and stood. Then she crossed her arms, too. "You can't scare me, Holt. I've been scared all my life. Now I'm through with that. And if you want to get rid of me quickly, which I can see you do, then the sooner we get started, the better. I have résumés out all over the country and I'm hoping something turns up soon, but that just means I need to work more quickly on the clinic. Besides, I'm on a bit of a deadline." She smiled down at her stomach.

He blew out a breath and tried not to think about the baby. His chest went tight and he found it difficult to breathe when he thought about babies. Everything hurt, and he wanted to pound his fists into a wall when the subject came up. The fact that Kathryn was pregnant definitely made this whole situation so much worse than it would be otherwise. And the fact that she was so mouthy?

It made him want to kiss that mouth closed.

He scowled.

"Stop frowning at me and give in to the inevitable," she said. "The sooner you do what I want, the sooner I'll go away."

"You know, somehow I don't remember you being this annoying, Kathryn."

To his surprise, she laughed. "You don't remember me at all, do you?"

"A little. You had big eyes and you were very…"

"Intense. I was intense."

"Wistful. And thin. As if a puff of wind would blow you away."

"Well, that certainly won't happen now, will it?"

"You're not exactly a giant." He couldn't help smiling.

"I'm big enough." Somehow he didn't think she was talking about physical size.

"All right, I'll be more cooperative, and I won't ignore your emails and phone calls. And lists. What exactly do you want?"

"For one thing, I want your assurance that you'll be at the town meeting."

"Town meeting?"

She drew a folded-up piece of paper out of her purse. He looked at it.

"It's not my best work," she admitted, gesturing toward the paper announcing that there would be a meeting at the community center on Friday to discuss the clinic. "But when I discovered that we could use the community center Friday and that I could use the mayor's copier, I wanted to get the announcements out right away. I've placed them in every shop and public building."

A note of uncertainty slipped into her voice as he stared at the pristine and very professionally worded bit of paper.

"I'm a little nervous," she said. "When I lived here before, I didn't get to know anyone well. What if people think I'm some city girl over-stepping my boundaries? A lot of the people who need the doctor the most are the older ones, but they might not show up at the meeting. For that matter, the younger ones might not, either. This isn't exactly an exciting topic. What if no one comes?"

Holt frowned. He wanted to go back to two weeks ago when he knew Kathryn only as some hazy memory. Now he knew she had a history and fears and a sense of responsibility. She was set on helping Larkville, and the Double Bar C was wedded to the town.

"They'll come," he promised. "And yes, *I'll* come."

"Thank you."

"For agreeing to go to the meeting?"

"And for the lesson on calf vaccination."

He smiled, but as he turned to go, his smile disappeared. She had one hand on her back.

"You're doing it again," he said.

She turned back. "What?"

"Your back? I know you're pregnant, but does this happen often?"

"More often lately, because, well, I'm bigger and it's a bit of a strain. It's nothing."

But after his father and Hank, he knew how nothing could turn into something. "Wes," he called, and Wes Brogan, who was the foreman of the Double Bar C, looked up. "Finish up without me, all right?"

"Not a problem, Holt."

"What do you think you're doing?" Kathryn asked as Holt took her by the elbow and started to lead her toward his truck. He tried not to notice her soft skin beneath his fingertips.

"I don't think you should drive. I especially don't think you should drive that thing you've been driving. I've seen it."

"I'm fine."

Holt counted to ten in his thoughts. "Okay, you're fine. Humor me, darlin'. I just agreed to come to your meeting and I'm all kinds of cranky about that. Those color-coded little lists of yours put me in a bad mood. I'm especially not partial to pink." He made sure his tone was teasing, but he didn't let go of her.

"Are you…are you making fun of me?" she asked as she moved with him. She looked down at where his hand was firmly around her arm. For a second she stumbled.

He caught her more firmly to him, even though that meant she was now wedged up against him and he could feel the curve of her hip. Holt wanted to groan.

Instead, he turned and grinned at her. "Make fun of you? I'd never do that, darlin'."

"Stop that."

"Stop what?" He kept moving her toward his truck.

"Stop doing that sexy cowboy thing. I told you I'm not into cowboys anymore."

"That you did, and I assured you that while

you are one very attractive woman, I'm not into relationships, either. On the other hand, I would never forgive myself if I let you drive down some lonesome road in that car and you got stuck out there alone. But I could see you were going to be kind of stubborn about the car and not easy to lead at all. Kind of like those calves."

"A calf?"

Oh, good, she was mad. They were nearly to the truck.

"Only in temperament, you understand. You're a thousand times prettier than a calf. The point is that sometimes the only way to lead a calf is to distract it, even agitate it, and since the last thing you want is a cowboy, I figured that teasing you a bit might get you to be a bit more amenable to me calling the shots on this one thing."

She opened her mouth, no doubt to protest. He leaned closer. She was up against his truck now. He placed both hands on either side of her on the frame of the vehicle. "Get in the truck, Kathryn," he urged. "I know you don't want this, but I have limits. One of those limits is letting people get hurt."

And that was when his teasing ended, because he'd meant every word. "You're in pain. Your car isn't dependable. If you got hurt, it would be on my head. I'm driving you home, all right?"

She shut her mouth and nodded. Her movement sent her body brushing against his, and he wanted nothing more than to touch her. Instead, he forced himself to step away.

"Okay," she agreed quietly. "But if you ever compare me to a calf again, I will go onto the internet and tell the world that you are the least romantic cowboy ever."

Holt couldn't help himself then. He chuckled. "It's a deal, Kathryn." And that was how Holt ended up driving Kathryn all the way back to town.

"I'll have someone deliver your car to you later," he said. "After you see the doctor."

She turned toward him.

"Right," he said. "No doctor in town today. Austin it is."

She shook her head vehemently. "I don't need Austin. I've studied all the books. This pain is uncomfortable, but it's not labor. I'm just having Braxton Hicks. False labor. It will stop."

He swore, all traces of teasing gone.

She winced. "Sorry," she said when he looked at her. "Not a big fan of swearing. I've heard a lot of it."

"Want to explain that?"

"No. It's different with you. Cowboys probably swear a lot."

He smiled slightly. "They might." Then he drove on in silence. They were almost to town when he asked the question that had been bugging him.

"How do you know it's not real labor?"

"Timing. The pain's not regular enough. That's the benefit of working for a doctor. Dr. Cooper keeps up a running commentary. Knowing I'm not close to a hospital, he's made sure I know what to expect and when I need to get to the hospital. It's not yet."

"You still have two weeks?"

"That's the estimated due date."

"Estimated?"

"Could be later. It's my first."

He felt as if a huge weight had been lifted from his shoulders. "Later? Good."

He noticed that she didn't look directly at him. How certain was she about the timing of her due date? It really wasn't his business, was it? None of this was. But…

"So, you're sure you're safe?" he couldn't seem to stop himself from asking.

"You won't have to deliver my baby."

He swiveled his head to stare her down. She had the good grace to look guilty. "I'm joking, okay?"

He still felt like hell.

"Holt?"

"Okay," he agreed, but he knew he sounded grumpy.

"I'm really sorry I made light of you having to deliver my baby. I know that wouldn't top your list of things to do."

"I'm fine."

Which was a bald-faced lie. Despite his teasing her earlier, he wasn't fine. He'd spent a lifetime learning the merits of levelheadedness, measuring his words, keeping his thoughts to himself, never letting himself be ruled by emotion. His parents' situation had been a good example of why those were handy lessons and he'd learned them well. In fact, he'd pretty much had the emotion weaned out of him, and he knew he'd hurt women who had expected what he couldn't provide.

As for Lilith, she'd grown to hate him for not having been that romantic cowboy figure she'd wanted. When she'd gotten pregnant despite taking precautions, she hadn't even told him. Instead, she'd made arrangements to give their baby away. And when he found out…things had gotten so much worse. Hellish. Then, just when he'd settled back to concentrating only on the one thing that never made him feel out of step—the ranch—Kathryn had showed up. Suddenly he was back to staring all his deficiencies in the face, being on his guard. Here was another pregnant woman thinking he was more than he really was.

Thank goodness she was leaving soon. But until then, he wasn't going to have her health or the health—no, the *life*—of her baby on his con-science. And he would not apologize for being a Neanderthal about the whole thing. Kathryn had brought all this to his doorstep. That made him mad as fire.

And he still wanted to kiss her. All night long.

Holt was almost to the house, but Kathryn couldn't help noticing that he was gripping the steering wheel as if he wanted to choke it to death. She probably shouldn't have let him drive her home. She'd promised herself that she'd never let another person order her around. And it hadn't even been his manipulative, sexy teasing that had changed her mind. Frankly, his touch had made her feel embarrassingly wanton for a pregnant woman, so her instinct had been to run before she did something really dumb. But beneath the sexy cowboy act, she could see that he was re-ally worried and that was why she'd agreed to the ride. Holt had faced serious illness and death re-cently, and the ghosts of those experiences must still be with him. Besides, much as she wanted to be totally independent and do the breezy "I'm fine, the baby's fine" routine, sometimes being pregnant and alone was terrifying.

And Holt, even when he was annoyed and wishing her in Hades, made her feel as if nothing disastrous could happen when she was with him. Not that she would tell him so. After all he'd been through with his father and friend, he probably didn't need to have her and her baby's welfare on his conscience. She'd tried to relieve him of any sense of responsibility. It hadn't worked. Time to try a different tactic to distract him from her situation.

"Before you leave, I want to talk about the meeting," she began.

He stopped crushing the wheel and looked at her. "You're in pain and you want to discuss a boring meeting?"

"See? That's what I mean. If even you think it's boring and you're one of the chairmen of the clinic committee, no one's going to want to come."

He blinked and bore down on the accelerator

a bit too hard. "I am not one of the chairmen of the committee. This wasn't my idea."

"But you're on board now."

He didn't answer that. "I told you they'd come."

She chose not to answer *that*. "I need to find some way to make it fun."

He rolled his eyes. "Will there be football?"

"What?"

"Hon, this is Texas. You may not have lived here long-term, you may not really be a Texas gal, but if you're talking Texas and fun, you're talking football or rodeo or sex."

Kathryn rolled her eyes. "Now you're just mocking me. You know Texas isn't that—that caricature."

"Maybe not, but now you're annoyed and not so worried. Stop trying to make it fun. You're talking about a clinic. You're not offering pony rides. Trust me, they'll come."

"But—"

"Trust me."

"I'm not real good with trust issues. I've been betrayed before."

She felt him glance her way. "You want to

explain that in greater detail than you already have?" There was an edge to his voice.

She shut her mouth. She'd said too much, letting that little fact pop right out without thinking. There was too much shame attached to her marriage, and she was sorry she'd mentioned it. "Not a chance."

They drove on in silence. "We still have to discuss your part of the meeting," she finally said.

"*My* part?"

"Yes. People look up to you as a leader in the community. I have friends, but most people will listen to you more than they will a woman who isn't staying. I want you to speak at the meeting."

"I hate public speaking."

"Why am I not surprised?"

"And if you're looking for fun, putting me at a podium will pretty much defeat your purpose."

"Maybe so, but people idolize you. If I don't have fun, I at least have you. You're the star attraction."

He swore again.

"Stop that. When the baby gets here, I don't want her to pick up bad habits."

"Me and the baby aren't going to be tight. We're not going to be anything. We may never even meet."

"I know. That was a knee-jerk reaction. Because you were being difficult."

"Let's be truthful. I'm being a jackass."

"Okay, you are. But I'm not giving up. I need you to speak. Have I mentioned how important this clinic is?"

"I know. People might die if it doesn't get built."

His voice had gone low and harsh.

"Let's not dwell on that part. But please, Holt. Just earlier today, you told me you'd cooperate more and I need you to do this. If you don't give the clinic your stamp of approval, it won't happen. People know I've been after you. If you come and just glower in the background, people will think you're not on board. Then no one else will be, either. This is going to be expensive. We need everyone's cooperation and support. Tell me you'll say a few words to let them know you want this thing."

Holt let out a sigh. "I promised, so I'll do it. Now, will you stop nagging if I speak?"

"Yes."

"All right, then."

"Thank you, Holt," she said primly. "Just so you know, I may distribute a few new fliers with your name on it. Maybe that will bring people in."

"You won't need that. They'll come."

"Why are you so certain? Would you come voluntarily if I wasn't nagging you?"

"I would go to the far side of the earth before I'd show up if I didn't need to be there. But I'm not the people of Larkville. I know them. They'll come to your meeting, even without football."

"Okay."

"Good. Kathryn?"

"Yes?"

"This isn't going to end it, is it? You're going to ask me to do more, aren't you?"

"If you'd really read all my lists, you would know. And you would have already done some things."

"I did some things. I put out some calls to people who might help," he said as he parked the truck in front of her house.

"You didn't tell me that!" She turned toward him quickly, despite her bulk.

"Whoa! Don't do that. And I didn't tell you because nothing has panned out yet. I told some friends who know people who know people in the medical field. That's how it works. Eventually I'll hear something, good or bad."

"Why not go straight to the source?"

"Because that's not how it works."

"You want to explain that?"

"No."

She could see she wasn't going to get any more out of him. And he had been right. The sudden move had made her back ache more. She refused to rub it, though, not with Holt here. This conversation may have made him forget why he was driving her home, but that laser vision that probably made him a good rancher would no doubt quickly have him turning all his attention to her pain if she wasn't careful.

"Don't worry, Kathryn," he said. "We'll get this done."

And over with, she imagined him thinking. She was sure he wanted her out of his hair. Well, she would be glad when they were done, too, because that crush she'd had when she was young didn't seem to have completely faded away.

The thought startled her and she quickly reached to open her door. "Don't move," Holt said. He got out of the truck and came around to her side. When he opened the door, he didn't wait for her to get out. Instead, he reached in, slid one arm beneath her knees and lifted her out.

"Holt?"

"What?"

"What are you doing?" His arms were around her. Her heart was pounding hard.

"I'm making sure you don't nudge anything loose before I get to make a fool of myself at your meeting."

And with that he carried her into her house and laid her on her bed, her body sliding against his. Then he ordered her to stay in bed and left her staring after his departing broad back.

Kathryn was left sputtering. She hadn't even gotten a chance to remind him that she didn't allow any man to run her life anymore. She would tell him next time.

But first she had to try to forget how it had felt to have been held against Holt's chest.

CHAPTER SIX

HOLT swore at himself all the way home. Kathryn was playing serious havoc with his senses. She was going to drive him insane before they were through. These past few years he'd had to deal with losses that still haunted him. He'd learned how destructive emotions could be and he'd faced adversity, but there was something about Kathryn that made him think that she had the ability to really mess him up for good.

He had to stay detached. And when the clinic project was on its way…

Then we're done. Thank goodness. Feeling personally responsible for the health and welfare of an entire town…man, he hated that feeling.

Worrying that Kathryn might start having the right kind of pains in the wrong time and place—*that* made him totally crazy.

Probably because he didn't want her to be his

business, or for there to be anything personal between them.

That didn't mean he hadn't noticed how achingly soft she'd been when he'd held her in his arms. And when she'd shifted against him, it had taken all his strength not to lower his head and devour that pretty pink mouth.

Which was just more proof that he needed to be careful. Kathryn would be bad for him, but he would be much worse for her. He needed to maintain even more control than usual.

So stick to what you're good at. Cattle. Horses. Stay away from what you're bad at. Women. Babies. Lilith had told him that someone so emotionally challenged wasn't built for fatherhood, and she'd been right.

There could be no more thinking about Kathryn's lips, he thought as a vision of Kathryn in his arms slipped into his mind, and heat seared him like a brand.

Darn the woman! Or, maybe darn himself. Still, one thing was certain. He would fulfill his promise to speak at her meeting, but his father had been the public speaker, not him. He was fine with small talk, with work talk, but he didn't make heartfelt speeches, so he would do this his way. That would probably plant a solid barrier between himself and Kathryn. Good.

Kathryn arrived at the community center a half hour early, but there were already a number of people there. Jess Jameson, Holt's sister, and her husband, Johnny, were in the front row. As was Jed Jackson, the county sheriff, and his new wife, Ellie, Holt's newly discovered half sister from New York—Clay's daughter from his first marriage. Mrs. Best had snagged an aisle seat and Sarah Anderson, who was in charge of the greatly anticipated Larkville Fall Festival, was just coming in the door. This year the festival was being held in honor of Holt's father, Clay, and was yet another reminder of how beloved the Calhouns were in the town. Ava was also there. She waved and smiled. Kathryn smiled back and noted that Dr. Cooper had, as usual, flown to California for his weekend trips to locate a house. But Dr. Cooper wasn't the only one missing.

Holt was nowhere in sight. As more minutes passed, panic began to blossom inside of her.

Still, she couldn't let anyone see that. Holt or no Holt, the show had to go on. And there was still time. She moved to the front where a podium had been set up and opened her folder of notes. Her plan was to do a general intro and then let Holt do the home-boy routine, talking to the neighbors he'd known all his life in a more personal way than she could. She'd tried to get hold of him several times this week and when that had proved impossible, she had left a phone message for him, outlining his part of the meeting. His only response had been a message he'd left on Dr. Cooper's phone after hours. His exact words were "I got the message."

That alone had been disconcerting. Hearing Holt's deep voice booming out of the speaker when she had expected her usual patients' messages telling her their reasons for needing an appointment had caught her by surprise. She had immediately remembered him carrying her to her house and dropping her on her bed. Suddenly all she could think of was Holt in her bedroom, and to her consternation, she'd blushed.

Unfortunately, she hadn't been alone. Luann Dickens had been in the office and had immediately wanted to know what messages Kathryn and Holt had been sharing. She had looked at Kathryn's stomach as if he might be the father.

"This baby is legitimate, Luann," Kathryn had wanted to say, or "I was in another state and married when this baby was conceived and I have not had nor do I intend to have sex with Holt Calhoun." But neither of those was appropriate when she was Dr. Cooper's receptionist and Luann was a patient. "The message was about the town meeting," she had stammered, then cursed herself for stammering.

"Hey, any meeting with Holt is a good meeting," Luann had said. "Just as long as you don't get too serious. Every woman wants him. No woman ever gets him. Or if she does, she doesn't get much of him and never for long. He's not into romance." It sounded as if Luann had attempted to catch Holt herself.

"It's business," Kathryn had answered primly.

But even she had to acknowledge that there was definitely something about Holt that made a woman think beyond business. She hated the fact that she, who knew better, was just as susceptible as Luann, who was always trolling for men. Maybe they weren't all that different.

But I have to be different, Kathryn had reminded herself. *I can't go around wondering what Holt looks like when he peels his shirt off at night. I have a baby to think about. It can't ever just be about me. I won't be like my parents or my ex-husband.*

Now, remembering Holt's brief message, Kathryn frowned. It was obvious that there were limits to how far she could push Holt just as there were limits to how much time she could safely spend in his presence. With her overactive hormones, she could easily forget to be smart around him.

Now she tried her best to look and *be* smart. But as she glanced through her notes, two things happened. Holt walked in the door, causing all eyes to turn. And right after that, a group of men came in, set up tables in the back of the room and began putting out huge platters of food. Barbecue, coleslaw, potato salad, more. The aroma was enticing, wonderful. Not on tonight's agenda. But the people filing in didn't look surprised. In fact, some of the women came bearing cakes and pies.

What was going on? Kathryn started toward the back where people were entering in twos and threes, but she spotted the mayor and made a beeline toward her. "Johanna, is this courtesy of the town?"

Johanna smiled and shook her head. "This is courtesy of your partner."

Partner? Was that what Holt was? "I didn't know anything about it."

Johanna shrugged. "The only reason I know is because I was in Gracie May's Diner just as they were loading up the truck."

"But…"

"Kathryn, relax. Holt has his own way of doing things. Always has. Always will. And he isn't one to talk about his plans."

Well, that was for sure. Getting the man to cooperate was like trying to drag a mule. Or at least what she imagined dragging a mule was like. The man always seemed to be in control.

And she was a woman who had promised herself she wouldn't be managed by someone like that.

Kathryn turned toward Holt. She had no idea why Gracie May's Diner was serving food at this meeting or why she hadn't been told. What she knew was that if she and Holt were partners, he should be sharing a lot more with her than he had been up to this point.

But when she started in his direction, she quickly found that she was not alone in her desire to talk with Holt. She was still six feet away from him when a man snagged Holt's attention. "Holt, you're just the man I've been dying to talk to. I need some good horse advice," the man said.

"Ed, you don't want me. You want Johnny."

"Yes, I mean to talk to Johnny, too, of course. He's the horse whisperer, but your daddy always helped me out in the past, and the way I see it, you inherited his genes and his horse sense and I wouldn't ever buy a horse without the Calhoun stamp of approval."

Kathryn watched as Holt took a pen and a scrap of paper from his pocket and scribbled something. "All right, I'll find a few spare hours to ride out with you and give you my opinion," he promised the man.

A few feet farther someone else stopped him. Kathryn could tell by the woman's intense expression that she was concerned about something and by the way she walked away looking relieved that Holt had helped her. He made another note on the paper. It quickly became apparent to Kathryn that Holt, who as the quarterback of the football team and a Calhoun had always been looked up to, had now been elevated to the level of Santa Claus. He solved problems. He was the go-to guy for the people of the town. He had been gone for a long time helping a dying man. He had agreed—reluctantly—to help *her*.

And—she looked toward the tables—he had provided food for the masses. Without talking to her. Not that it was a terrible thing, of course, but…

There was no more time to think about it. The clock chimed seven and Kathryn looked toward Holt. He glanced toward the standing-room-only crowd and gave her a look that said, what?

Kathryn didn't know, but having those dark eyes turned on her made her feel far too aware that she was a woman.

Too bad. She'd already played that game when she was sixteen, and it had not turned out well. Luann Dickens was right. Holt wasn't a man a woman should be too attracted to unless she was prepared for some serious heartbreak.

Kathryn tucked that thought away. Giving him a slight nod and moving to the podium, she was very conscious of the fact that she had returned to town defeated, divorced and pregnant, and that the few people who knew her by more than sight probably also knew that she was here only for a short time. Nervously, she cleared her throat.

"Thank you for coming." Her voice was a whisper. She cleared her throat again. "I'm sure you know that Dr. Cooper is leaving, the clinic needs rebuilding and Larkville will need a new doctor. We're here to talk about how we can make that happen."

She thought she heard someone whispering that they had come to eat, but maybe that was her imagination.

"It will be costly," she admitted, amid some scowls and shaking of heads. "But it's important." She wanted to list the reasons why, but she knew that a native son would make a bigger impact. Especially if the native son was almost a god to the townspeople.

So, after the briefest of comments explaining the situation, she turned toward Holt. "Mr. Calhoun will explain what we're up against, what our options are and how we can make this happen." That was what she had included on Holt's list when she'd mentioned *his* part. Of course, she had given him many suggestions on things he might mention during his talk.

"Thank you for listening," she ended to polite applause. A few friends and acquaintances, including Mrs. Best and Ava, clapped much more enthusiastically.

"Good idea," Luann said. Warmth stole through Kathryn. When she'd been here years ago, her parents' reclusive ways had set her apart and she hadn't had real friends.

But when the polite applause faded to silence and Holt stepped onto the stage, the crowd went wild. There was hooting and hollering and boot stomping. "You tell us, Holt," some man called out.

Holt had removed his hat and his dark hair shone in the light. Standing on the small stage, his shoulders seemed broader, his legs longer. He didn't disappear behind the podium or take out any paper.

"Not much to say here. You all heard what Kathryn said. She's 100 percent right and that's a fact. We need a doctor and a clinic. You can probably figure out the reasons why. Does anyone have a problem with that?"

Everyone looked around. No one spoke.

"Good. Then we'll do it. I'll help. You'll help. Kathryn will tell you how it's going to get done. If you're uncertain of the reasons why, she has a list that will clear things up for you. Listen to what she has to say because this is important. Then, when she's through and you're all on board, we'll celebrate." He nodded toward the tables in the back. Then he stepped off the stage.

Kathryn looked at him in disbelief. He had been up on the stage less than a minute. He stared her straight in the eye, challenging her. What was she going to do?

What could she do? She couldn't chastise Holt right here in front of his adoring fans. They would probably run her out of town. So, she gave him a tight smile. Then she moved back on stage and began listing the reasons the clinic was needed, using all the arguments she had used on Holt. She told them what would be involved.

"This is a project that the community has to get behind, but it's an important one. You've gotten used to having a clinic—there are those who depend on it and none of us ever knows when it will be our turn. I'm not at liberty to discuss individual cases, but working in Dr. Cooper's office, I've seen people in pain, people who would suffer if they didn't get immediate medical attention." She gave more real-life examples and, despite herself, tears threatened. She fought them back. She didn't want to be accused of using people or trying to gain their cooperation by using her own scary situation as a ploy. Finally, she ran out of arguments. "So, I hope that after you've had a chance to review the facts, you'll all agree to support this project," she ended. "Are—are there any questions?"

One woman raised her hand. "Will Holt be working on this?"

This time Kathryn managed not to blush. She wasn't sure if the woman was interested in him romantically or if she simply believed that Holt could move mountains. Kathryn was no longer so sure that he could move mountains. After all, he hadn't done half of what she'd asked him to do tonight. No way was she answering the question for him.

She turned to him. "Holt?"

He almost glowered at her. "I said I would help. I meant that I would help in whatever way I'm needed."

The woman smiled. "I was pretty sure of that. You always do the right thing."

"That's Holt. Always there to lend a hand or give some good advice," another man said.

Kathryn gritted her teeth. "Well, then, any more questions?"

"Nope," Johnny said. "Holt's on board. That's good enough for me." She wondered if he had been coached to say that, or if it was really true. He *was,* after all, Holt's brother-in-law.

"Good enough for me, too," Mrs. Best chimed in. A chorus of voices agreed.

The mayor stood. "Well, then, if there's nothing more…" She looked at Kathryn, who shook her head. "I'd say that you've all earned a meal."

Immediately there was applause and people began moving toward the back. Holt remained near the front of the room. As if he knew Kathryn wouldn't be happy until she spoke to him.

"You didn't tell me that you were going to bribe them with food," she said.

"Don't sound so prissy, Kathryn. You were concerned that no one would show up, and I told you they would. A little barbecue never hurt anyone."

"I know that. It was actually a good idea, but couldn't you have at least told me about it? Or that you didn't intend to talk about any of the things on my list."

"I think I might have mentioned before that I'm not one to get emotional. This needed emotion. You were the one to supply that."

She sucked in her breath. "I like to think that I'm professional."

He smiled. "You are that. Kind of prissy about it, too."

She frowned at him.

He raised a brow. "Not that there's anything wrong with prissy."

"I like being in control."

"It shows. And you were."

But she was no fool. "They came because of you. Or your food. Or both. And they agreed to go along because you were involved."

He shrugged. "Give them credit. They might not have jumped as soon as you wanted them to jump, but they're not unreasonable people."

"They expect a lot of you. You like being Santa Claus?" she asked.

"As an owner and manager of the biggest money-making concern in the area, I have obligations, and I don't shirk them."

"Is that what this clinic is? An obligation?"

"I have my reasons for doing this. So do you. The people at the clinic. Your baby. Your job."

Kathryn had watched him selflessly giving of

his time. She also knew something else. "But some of my reasons seem selfish."

"No. They're logical. You're human."

"Maybe I'm just scared," she admitted. "A job will keep me from being vulnerable. I can't be vulnerable."

He gave her a long look, and she knew that she had said too much. Fortunately, Holt didn't seem to want to discuss her vulnerable side any more than she did.

"Understood," he said. "And I'll do what's needed, but I won't be what I'm not."

"Which is…"

"The kind of man who operates on an emotional level. So don't expect me to get up on a stage or anywhere else. Don't expect me to share secrets or tell you everything I'm thinking. I never was and never will be that guy."

"All right," she said. And he walked away. Within seconds, the crowd had glommed on to him. She was alone. But then she always had been. That was the way it would be from here on. Her and her baby. She would make a home for them. A life. And men like Holt would never have any say in that world or any power to hurt her.

If truth be told, she was probably the only woman in Larkville who was glad that Holt wasn't an emotional man. It made him safe.

Or at least saf*er*. Didn't it?

CHAPTER SEVEN

HAD there ever been a woman so determined to be strong who looked as fragile as Kathryn did? Holt found himself turning the question over in his mind for the rest of the meeting. She had been upset with him for not letting her in, but he wasn't a committee kind of guy.

Stop kidding yourself, Calhoun. It's not the committee that makes you uncomfortable. It's Kathryn. It was simple, really. He found her attractive. More than attractive. That he could have dealt with, but he also found her intriguing. She'd come back to Larkville a bit beaten up, and here in a town where she'd apparently been an unknown she was going to make her stand, do some good, rebuild her world and rise from the ashes like a phoenix. A phoenix who would soon fly away with her baby and never return.

Remember that, he told himself. He'd already

played this scene before. Lost people. Lots of people, but most importantly, a woman. A baby.

And she wanted to be short-term partners with him. No question about it, Kathryn was dangerous. With her passion and her demands, her temporary stature and her baby on the way, she was everything he should be avoiding.

That wasn't happening. He'd given his word. He'd set wheels in motion and he would continue right through to the end. But if he spent too much time in Kathryn's presence he was going to kiss her. He might even lose control and let kissing lead to more. The only way to avoid that was to take a big step back and do his helping from a distance.

That should work. It would at least make sure that no life-changing mistakes were made.

Okay, she got it, Kathryn thought the next day. Holt wasn't going to be led, and he didn't want to spend time with her. That was good, wasn't it? Because she didn't want to spend much time with him, either.

If she did, sooner or later he would disappoint her.

The thought made her smile. *You mean he hasn't disappointed you yet?* she asked herself.

The answer was complicated. He hadn't let her lead him where she wanted him to go, but he *had* produced the results she'd wanted. So she probably should back off, tell him what she was doing and simply wait for him to produce results on his end.

"All right, let's begin," she murmured, staring at the keyboard. There wasn't even any point in wondering if Holt was into social networking. The very thought would probably have those dark eyes turning icy and dangerous. But he was still a businessman. She addressed an email to him. It read:

Results of the meeting. Two hundred people in attendance. All in favor of moving ahead. Now we fundraise. Ideas?

When no response appeared within a few hours, she wrote another. All it said was:

Please?

Five minutes later, she got a response.

Don't do that.

Do what?

Beg. You know how I feel about begging.

I wasn't. I was asking nicely.

I'm not nice. Just say what you want.

I did. You ignored me.

I'm running a ranch here.

I know, but...

All right. You want a progress report. I've contacted a friend who has contacted a friend who is an instructor at a well-known medical college in Chicago. He's sending out feelers. As for the fundraiser, that's outside my comfort zone.
I'll come up with some ideas.

That would be best.

And then I'll run them past you.

You should know that I'll probably say yes to anything.

Even if it's something that might be embarrassing for you?

Are you baiting me?

Maybe she was, Kathryn thought. It occurred to her that even though she was enjoying this time in Larkville much more than the last, and even though everyone in town had been nice to her—they smiled at her on the street, the patients brought her cookies and oohed and aahed over her expanding girth—she didn't really spend any time socializing. Maybe that was because she was afraid of making friends she'd have to leave behind. Her house wasn't that close to other houses because her parents had been sticklers for privacy and they had looked down on the citizens of Larkville. There were empty lots on either side of her and an empty field across the road. Holt was one of the few people she talked to on a regular basis outside of work.

So, yes, maybe she was enjoying this exchange too much. Maybe she *was* messing with him a bit.

She was also starting to experience major pains. Long, undulating waves of pain that made it feel as if her entire body was pulsing, contracting, hurting.

"It'll go away," she thought. She hoped. And it did…until it came back and hunted her down.

She doubled over and panic filled her soul.

Holt waited for Kathryn's response. And waited.

Nothing happened. And he didn't even consider that she had simply decided to be an ass like him and was making him wait. That wasn't Kathryn's way. She was gung ho all the way. If she wasn't responding, there was a reason.

He called her. The phone rang three times. Four. The machine picked up. The beep finally sounded.

"Kathryn, pick up. It's Holt," he ordered.

Silence. Eventually the machine cut off.

He dialed again, and now his muscles felt tight,

his heart was pounding the way it had when his father had collapsed. "Kathryn, answer the damn phone. I need to talk about—about the fundraiser." He paused. She still didn't answer. "And I'm coming over. To talk about the fundraiser," he lied.

The phone clicked as the receiver was lifted. "Holt? Don't…don't come. It's not a good time." Her voice was too soft, the words too halting. "It's…it's really…"

Holt heard a distinct gasp and then a moan. "Your back? Braxton Hicks?" he asked.

Silence.

"Kathryn? Talk. Now," he ordered.

He knew something was wrong when she didn't instantly inform him that she wasn't into controlling men like him. "I— Braxton Hicks?" she said. "No. I don't…think so. I don't know." He could hear her breath coming and going. That was bad. Very bad.

"If you don't know, then it's time to go to the hospital and find out."

More silence.

He cursed the distance and the phone and this inadequate way of communicating. "Kathryn?"

"Yes, I will," she promised. "I'll go now." Her voice started to fade and he could tell she was going to hang up.

"Dammit, no! Stop. Do not hang up the phone. And above all, don't get into that car. That's an order. You can't drive. Don't even think about it."

"I— All right, no, I can't drive. I started thinking about this last week, but then…I'm going to go ask Johanna."

"No. You're not. Johanna may be an excellent mayor, but she drives like total crap. And besides, it's too far. Don't move. I'm coming to get you."

"I can't let you do that."

He wanted to ask why, but all this talk was wasting time. "Watch me. I guarantee I'll have you to Austin in no time."

Then he jogged out to the hangar and jumped into his helicopter.

Holt came through the door looking like one of those guys in a movie, the ones that come walking out of the fog. The ones that come to save the day when all was lost.

And Kathryn was ready to follow him anywhere, because she had never envisioned what this pain would be like. It was like nothing she'd ever experienced. It was eating her alive. And she had to bear it. She had to do everything she was supposed to in order to make sure her baby's health wasn't compromised, but when the pain came in waves, the urge to sink to her knees or to curl up in a ball was fierce.

The thing was, she had tried both, and neither one of them did a thing to cut the pain.

But Holt would get her to the hospital. Just as he'd made sure people came to the meeting, he would make sure she got to a safe place to give birth. Because that was what Holt did. He helped people in the most efficient way possible. His way. Not their way, but the job got done nonetheless.

"Do you have everything you need?" he asked.

She nodded, reaching for a small bag she had packed weeks ago.

He beat her to it, scooping up the bag. "You're ready?"

"Yes." It was all she could get out as the waves of pain returned and she felt herself blanching, being sucked under. Pain that beat her down, threw her around and pummeled her, overwhelming her.

Holt lifted her as if she was nothing. Weightless. His long strides took them outside and across the street to the empty field. The contraction began to subside.

"This probably wasn't on your agenda today," she said weakly as he placed her in the helicopter and strapped her in.

"Always plan for the unexpected," he said. "That's life on a ranch. This isn't going to ruin my day."

But she could tell that he was tense. His jaw was locked, his words, comforting as they were, were clipped. "I wish I had someone to take care of you while I fly, but you'll simply have to rely on the sound of my voice," he warned.

To her surprise she still had the strength to

laugh. A little. "You've never wanted to talk before."

"Anyone can rattle nonsense. It takes practice to be a sullen uncommunicative jackass," he told her. "I'll do my best."

"Did you…did you just make a joke?" she asked. But then the pain returned.

"Be still," Holt ordered. "Breathe. Breathe. Watch me while I fly. Concentrate on me and breathe." The noise of the propeller was loud, but she could still hear every word as he bit them off.

She focused on his hands on the controls. Long, lean fingers. She stared. She breathed. Occasionally a tiny gasp would escape her.

His hands tightened on the controls.

"I'll—I'll try not to do that again," she said.

He swore beneath his breath. "You do whatever you like. If you want to swear or scream or tell me what you really think of me, now would be a good time to let loose. I won't judge you or remind you of it later."

"I don't like yelling," she said. "My parents were yellers. My husband was a major yeller. And—"

"Yes, I've been known to swear the house down

when I'm angry," he said. "So, no yelling. What did you do when all this yelling was going on?"

"Hid. Cowered. Cried. I wasn't equipped to fight back. Or at least I didn't know the right words to make it stop."

He didn't respond.

"Too much information," she said. "More than I should have revealed."

"I don't share secrets. It's not going further than me. You've got no reason to worry."

"I'm not. I'm not. I'm—"

"Almost there, Kathryn. Hang on. Stay with me. Concentrate on me. Tell me, when all that yelling was going on, what did you want to say?"

"Stop yelling. Stop bullying me. I'm a person, too. I count. This is a baby. It's mine, it's yours. How can you not want it? Why are you so angry?"

Kathryn's voice had risen on the last words. She was practically yelling, but she felt the thud as Holt set the helicopter down. Immediately medical personnel appeared. He must have called ahead to let them know they were on their way.

She was placed in a wheelchair. A nurse started

to wheel her away. Kathryn looked up at Holt. "I— Thank you."

He nodded and started to walk away. "Will there be someone with her?" he asked the nurse.

"We'll monitor her closely and check her often."

"But some of the time she'll be alone."

"Until it's time for the heavy lifting."

Kathryn thought she heard Holt say something, but the pain took hold again. A few minutes later she was in a birthing room. Holt was holding her hand. "Why are you still here?" she asked.

He ignored her. "Let's do this thing," he said.

She tried to smile. "I'm really grateful. I can see why people see you as the cowboy hero."

"Shut up, Kathryn," he said. And then he kissed her.

The shock, the zing, the utter insanity of it, lasted all the way to the next contraction. Having Holt here was… There was that safe feeling again.

But she could tell by the look on his face that this wasn't easy for him. That kiss had been a prime example of him trying to deal with the craziness of the moment. Holt hated emotion. His jaws were clenched. His big hand was locked around hers like a vise. His tan seemed almost pale.

But he held on and held her. Through contraction after contraction.

Eventually, though, the nurse told her that they were getting to the crucial moment, the part where Kathryn had heard that women screamed out their innermost thoughts. In fact, she'd already let loose with things she shouldn't have. Besides, Holt had borne enough. He didn't need to live through the really intense and emotional stuff. So when the doctor finally came in, Kathryn turned to Holt.

"It's tag team time. Thank you. I'll see you on the other side."

He opened his mouth to say something just as the pain came at her harder than ever. She sucked in a breath, trying to hold on.

"I want you to go. Now, Holt," she yelled. "A man got me into this, and I don't want you or any men in here." It was a total lie, but it did the trick. He left.

Somehow she stopped herself from begging him to come back.

* * *

Holt tried not to think about what was going on with Kathryn in the delivery room. Of course, he knew. On a ranch you learned the basics of reproduction at a very early age, but Kathryn was a woman. And she wasn't just a woman in pain. She was a sensitive woman. That much had been revealed during their conversation on the way here.

And though he had meant what he said about not revealing her words or holding them against her, he wasn't going to forget them, either. This was a woman who had been subjected to some situations that were none of his business. He especially didn't want to think about what she had said about her husband. No one knew better than he did that there were two sides to every story. The fact was that she was having a baby and her husband was nowhere in sight. What had happened and whose fault it was, if it was anyone's, was not his concern. But he knew two things.

Kathryn had been hurt and he was just the type of man who could hurt her more and hurt himself, too, if their lives got tangled up together. She was having a baby, and then she was taking that baby and moving to a city, while he wasn't sure if he could ever contemplate having a child again.

Still, during that time he'd been in the labor room with her hand in his—heck, with her lips beneath his—he'd known that hard as it might be to be present for the delivery of a child and all the painful memories that called up, he would have done it. Stayed until the end. He couldn't run. Or leave her alone here.

So Holt waited. And paced. And waited some more.

CHAPTER EIGHT

TIRED but alert after the birth of her daughter, Kathryn mentally thanked Holt and her years of running, in that order. Holt had kept her sane on the trip to the hospital and had gotten her here safely and in time. He'd held her terror at bay during her labor. For the rest, her athletic build had, the doctors told her, made this an easier delivery, if there was such a thing. At any rate, by the time she had decided that, yes, she might in fact want to be drugged, she was too far along. Which was why she was in less pain and wider awake than she would otherwise have been.

That was also why she knew the minute that Holt appeared in the hospital room doorway. He didn't come in, but just stood there filling up the space.

"You okay?" he asked.

"Never better." He was looking everywhere

but at her baby. Clearly he wasn't comfortable with babies, so this might be an awkward meeting. A little levity couldn't hurt. "I could climb a mountain."

"Maybe you could hold off on that until later," he suggested.

"Good idea. You might have to rescue me. I *am* a little bit worn out."

"Not surprising. Was it difficult? Were you all right? I could have stayed."

But Kathryn remembered how he'd looked, as if he was being chased by demons. "No offense, Calhoun, but you have quite a reputation when it comes to women. You've probably seen a lot of lady parts, and I wasn't eager to have you see mine under less than flattering circumstances," she teased, wanting to let him off the hook and lighten the tone. "Besides, I was just fine," she lied. At the time it had felt as if her entire body was under attack.

He studied her as if he could determine whether or not she was telling the truth.

"And anyway, I'm perfectly fine now," she told him.

"Which means it was pretty bad at the time." Yes, it had been. At the very end when the pain had made her a little crazy, she had almost asked a nurse to see if Holt was still around, but a woman bent on being independent wouldn't do that, and she had hung on alone.

"Holt, I'm good. Honest."

He looked at her as if he wanted to argue, but finally he blew out a breath. Then he raised that sexy eyebrow. "Lady parts?"

She did her best to look down her nose. "They're mine and I can call them whatever I want."

He touched two fingers to his forehead in a salute. "As you say."

A small noise came from the clear bassinet at Kathryn's side. Holt visibly tensed. He still hadn't looked at the baby, she noticed.

Now he looped his thumbs in his belt loops and glanced to the side. "I'm glad that you're okay." He turned to go, then turned back. "Let me know when you need a lift home. You have my number."

"Holt?"

He pivoted quickly. "Yes?"

"I want you to know that me having the baby doesn't change anything. As soon as I get back in form, which admittedly might take a week or two, I'm continuing with the project. That race to the hospital taught me just how badly this is needed. Not everyone has a Holt Calhoun, or a helicopter, at their disposal. And I have no idea how much time I have left."

"No rushing things. That's just the drugs talking."

"No drugs. It's me talking."

"But you're tired. We'll discuss this later."

"Are you trying to back out on me?"

He stared her down. "I'm trying to keep in mind that your life has changed."

"It has, but some things haven't. Okay?"

"Okay."

"And, Holt? Her name is Izzy. Short for Isabelle."

His gaze passed over Izzy and landed on Kathryn. "Get some rest, Kathryn. We'll talk later."

Then she was alone with her baby. She looked down into those unfocused, beautiful eyes. "He's not so bad, Izzy," she told her child, kissing her on the forehead. "Don't get your feelings hurt. I'm sure it's nothing personal."

But he definitely didn't like babies. At all.

Holt tried not to think about Kathryn, about Kathryn with a baby or about the baby. He remembered finding out what Lilith had done and his anger when he had confronted her about her plans to give away their child without even having informed him of…anything. She hadn't told him when she miscarried later, either, if that was really what had happened, but he remembered every word she'd said during the argument they'd had when he'd heard about it secondhand. The gist of the message had been that a man like him was so lacking emotionally that she would never want to have a child with him or give birth to a child who might inherit his disposition. And what child would want such a cold man for a father?

He had hated her that day, and had never forgotten her words. There was, unfortunately, truth in them. Because she wasn't the first person who had told him he was cold. His mother, despite urging him not to care too deeply, had in her later years lamented that he was too detached. His father told him that the men in his family probably weren't equipped to offer what women and kids needed. Hadn't other women cursed him for being a cold Calhoun male?

And here was Kathryn, a woman who had already been hurt by other insensitive people. Now she had an innocent baby.

His whole body felt wrong. Chilled. Pained. Maybe he should just tell her that he would donate most of the money she needed. He would finish this thing alone.

But he knew he wouldn't. She'd told him that this was her proving ground. She needed this accomplishment on her résumé. So, what he needed to do was make sure he did his part without overstepping into the tasks she'd laid out for herself.

One thing was for certain. He needed to keep his distance. As much as possible. The woman made him forget who and what he was. And she had eyes that made him want to gaze into them like some idiot with an actual heart.

He cursed his stupidity. And when he got back

to the ranch, he took an ax and attacked a pile of wood. It took him hours.

"Are you okay, Holt?" Nancy asked.

He grunted at her.

"Do you want dinner?"

"Can't. Work to do." He kept swinging the ax. *Izzy. What kind of a name was Izzy?* But he knew. It was the kind of name a romantic, sentimental, wistful woman gave her child. A woman who needed a lot.

He brought the ax down hard, and a piece of wood went flying and nearly hit him on the arm. He almost wished it had. It would be a distraction.

But eventually, the pile of wood played out. And even with all that chopping and smashing, he still couldn't forget what he'd felt when Kathryn had been in pain and so brave.

And he couldn't deny that he wanted to see her again. What was wrong with him? He knew better than to start anything. Or even try to.

I probably just feel responsible for her, he told himself. *If she's struggling to make ends meet, how well-equipped can she be to house a baby?*

* * *

Kathryn was tired. Izzy was the sweetest thing on earth. Her heart hurt just to look at her, fearing that something would happen to the tiny baby who seemed like a wonderful but frighteningly fragile gift. What's more, she kept seeing that guarded expression on Holt's face as he'd avoided her baby.

Well, so what? Lots of men—and women—weren't big on babies. No big deal. But between her thoughts of Holt, her worries about Izzy and Izzy's nighttime feedings, Kathryn wasn't sleeping. How did people stand all this stress and responsibility?

"Silly question. They stand it because they love."

Still, she needed to stop worrying and tend to some things. Dr. Cooper was getting by with a rolling group of stand-in receptionists, and her work at the newspaper was flexible enough that her not being there didn't hurt the paper. But she did need to get back to work so she could support herself and Izzy. And she needed to send out more résumés. And stop wondering when she would see Holt again, and…

"I need to just stop. Especially stop thinking about Holt," she whispered. But that wasn't easy. She couldn't help remembering how he had come to her rescue and had taken most of her fears away. Or that he seemed uncomfortable around her now.

She had received an email from him this morning.

Found a potential candidate. Will be traveling to Chicago to talk to him.

That was it. No *How are you? How are you feeling? When can we meet again?*

"He's cut us loose, Izzy." Probably that wild trip to the hospital and all her wailing and baring her soul had disgusted him. *Well, so be it. If that's the way it is, then I'm better off without him.*

But while she'd been recovering, he'd gotten a candidate for the new doctor position. Things were moving, and she had to move, too—on to the next step with the project and her life. She had received a phone interview for a job just yesterday. It hadn't panned out, but it proved that her résumé wasn't totally terrible. Things might happen. They might happen faster if she completed the project. She should finish with Holt. Fast.

Izzy was starting to whimper. Kathryn cuddled the baby close. Just as Izzy had stopped fussing and settled against Kathryn's shoulder, the silence contented and wonderful, the doorbell rang.

Kathryn jerked. Her heart nearly stopped. Then it started thudding wildly. Since she'd lived here, Holt had been the only person who had come to her door.

The urge to look in the mirror was intense. She resisted. For one thing, she knew she had dark circles under her eyes. For another, checking her appearance in the mirror would prove something bad, that she cared what Holt thought of her looks.

She opened the door. And found Jess Jameson standing there. The woman had a slightly sheepish expression on her face. "I'm so sorry I haven't been around sooner, Kathryn. And I—well, the thing is…I should have. Locked into our own lives, we haven't even given you a proper baby shower! But we've gotten together some things now. If that's all right."

Kathryn was uncomfortably aware that this was Holt's sister standing on her doorstep. She shook her head. "Please don't apologize. There's no need. I've had my head down and working, too. I— You really didn't have to do this."

"Of course we did. You've just had a baby! A lovely baby. And your arms are full. May I… bring these in?"

"I— Yes, of course. Thank you." Kathryn stepped back to let Jess in. The woman was carrying two shopping bags.

"I'll just leave them right here," Jess said. "There are some clothes, some diapers and…I don't know what else is in there. And besides baby things, I brought you some of my home-baked treats. My specialty, you know."

Kathryn knew. Jess ran her own bakery and her treats could make a person swoon with pleasure. "Thank you so much. You make the best baked goods I've ever eaten!"

"Well, a woman who's just had a baby deserves to pamper herself a little, I think." Then she looked at Izzy and practically sighed. "She is so darling. Just a little sweetheart. I'm hoping to give my little Brady a brother or a sister someday. And boy or girl, I hope that it ends up with Johnny's hair. That man has hair a woman loves running her fingers through, you know?"

Kathryn didn't think it would be a good idea to say yes. Jess might think that Kathryn was coveting her husband. Or at least his hair. Worse, she might suspect that it was really her brother's hair Kathryn was thinking about…which was the truth. And was embarrassing. Still…

"Johnny has very nice hair," she said weakly. "But he probably feels the same way about your hair. You might have to have one of each."

Jess laughed as Izzy gurgled happily. She had a nice laugh. And she had brought all these baby goodies. And delicious food from the bakery. And said nice things about Izzy. Tears sprang to Kathryn's eyes.

Immediately Jess looked concerned. "I'm so sorry. Did I come at a bad time?"

"No. You came at a perfect time. Don't mind

me. It's just all the hormones. I was simply thinking about how nice you were."

"Oh, hon," Jess said, giving both Kathryn and Izzy a bit of a group hug. "I'm the one who should be crying. I should have come before you even had the baby. We all should have thought of it. We knew you were pregnant, but we just—"

"You knew I wasn't planning to stay. Please don't apologize about not having a shower. I thought there was a chance I might be gone by the time Izzy was born, too. There was no reason you should have needed to help me when I might have been gone before it mattered."

Jess gave her a "get real" look. "That's not the way it works. Neighbors help neighbors even if they're temporary neighbors. I'm going to round up the troops and we're going to help make you a real nursery—even if it's only a temporary one."

Kathryn started. "I have a nursery."

Jess looked surprised. "You do? Let me see. Just so I know what you have and what you don't."

"It's just through here." Kathryn led the way. "But really, I don't expect you to—"

"You *do* have a nursery," Jess said, moving up to the little bassinet. "I thought— He said—"

"He?"

"Uh-oh."

"I assume we're talking about your brother."

"You weren't supposed to know."

"He put you up to this?"

"He might have hinted that a woman with a baby might need some things. He wasn't sure what those things were and—well, you know Holt—he isn't remotely comfortable around topics like this, so he just pushed the button and then acted like he didn't want to talk about it anymore. I completely agree with him, though, on you needing some stuff. You've done great, but if a few of us women put our heads together, we can make things even better."

"I don't want you being pushed into anything, or for anyone to feel obligated. I would hate that."

Jess held up one hand. "You're on the wrong track. Because while Holt may have been the impetus, he was right. And while Holt and I may be different, as Calhouns we share one trait. Once we get something in our heads, we follow through on it. We don't let go. I want to help. I intend to help. Let me?"

"I—Jess, what if I leave next week? I don't know when a job might show up."

"Then we pack up all of your stuff and you move on to your new life. With your new baby things. Come on, Kathryn. It'll be fun. Not just for you, but for me, too. I love shopping for baby things. Okay?"

Kathryn frowned. "I'm really not sure about this."

"You're getting a clinic and a new doctor for us."

"I haven't done it yet."

"You will. I don't really know you, but I know that you've got Holt."

That was a major overstatement. She didn't have—nor would she ever have—Holt.

"Please. Let us give back a little."

"Maybe just a little. For Izzy."

Jess smiled.

"Jess?"

"Yes?"

"I'm not sure when I'll see Holt again soon,

but tell him thank you. It was nice of him to do this when he's so uncomfortable around babies."

Jess looked at her. "I'll tell him, but I'll leave out the part about the baby."

"I'm sorry. I didn't mean—it wasn't criticism. Lots of people feel awkward around babies."

"It might be more than that with Holt."

Kathryn raised an eyebrow. And waited. Jess was shaking her head. "I probably shouldn't have said that. My hunch is pure speculation because Holt never discusses his personal life. I know women who have wanted him, but haven't been able to get him. I know women who may have dated him, but don't really have anything to show for it and nothing to tell. I don't know much more. My brother is a complete clam where his emotions are concerned. He's not a talker, not a sharer, and he's been like that all my life. So, all I'm basing my guess on is the fact that he was engaged to Lilith Kingston and then he wasn't engaged anymore. There was a big argument, and some people say that she was cheating on him, that she might even have been pregnant, but I don't know the details. She moved away, and he'll never volunteer that information. He'll probably take it to his grave. But just so you know, I'm sure Holt wouldn't harm a baby."

Kathryn blinked. "I would never think that. It doesn't matter that he's not into babies."

"It does. When a woman has a child, she wants the world to love her baby. It hurts when someone doesn't. But Holt is…Holt. He'll never change."

"I wasn't going to try. We're not that tight."

Jess studied her for a few seconds. Then she sighed. "It's just as well. I was thinking—a whole bunch of us were thinking—that you might be falling in love with him, but I guess it's good that you're not. You're going to leave, and Holt will never go. I'm afraid that he's tied to that ranch more than he ever will be to any woman. Maybe he tells his secrets to the cattle, but he sure doesn't share them with anyone else."

"He's a good man, though."

Jess laughed. "Of course. Holt's the best. He takes care of everyone."

Including me, Kathryn thought after Jess had gone. People had needs. Holt tended to them. He made light of it, but what a burden that must be.

She was going to have to make it clear that she was not going to need coddling.

It was time to jump back in with both feet and make it clear that she was in charge of getting a clinic built. *And I'm not even going to think about Holt as a man. At least, not anymore.*

She picked up the phone and dialed. Nancy patched her through. Holt's low, deep, sexy voice came on the line. Immediately Kathryn understood why all those women were always trying to get his attention.

"Something's wrong," he said.

"No. Yes. I just want you to know that I don't want you making me into a pet project."

"Don't have a clue what you're talking about."

She stalled. Felt embarrassed. Then remembered Jess's words.

"Good, then. Just keep thinking that way. I'm an independent woman. I know how to get things and get things done."

"Something get your back up, Kathryn?"

Other than the fact that his voice was making her think of rumpled sheets and things she shouldn't be thinking about?

"No. I'm good. I'm fine. I'm surviving. Not a thing wrong here. I don't need a thing. Nothing. At all."

"Right. Got that. Is that what you called to tell me? That you didn't need anything?" He sounded kind of angry.

"Well. Yes, I did. And one thing more. I'm ready to start up again."

Oh, Lord, that had sounded a bit sexual, hadn't it?

"On the clinic project," she amended. "I want to meet with you. Talk about it. Plan."

Was that a groan?

"Holt?"

"Still here. Kathryn, you just had a baby."

"I'm aware of that. It was two weeks ago. I need to move forward." So that she could move away from Holt and all the disturbing sensations he called up in her.

Silence. Then, "Okay. Let's get this done and over with."

Good. He wanted to end it, too. Why did that not feel good?

"When?"

"I'll be out of town tomorrow. The next day?"

"I'll be there."

"Not in that car."

"Yes."

"Kathryn."

"Holt. It's my life, my car, my world. Soon I'll be gone. I'll be driving all over creation in that car and you won't even think about it because I won't be in your life anymore. Get used to it. I'm driving my own car. It's safe." Well, reasonably safe, but she knew that it didn't look it. "And I have my cell phone. I just have to put some minutes on it."

"What the hell does that mean? Does it mean you don't really have a phone?"

Kathryn bristled. For a second there, Holt had sounded the way James used to when he decided that she wasn't the sort of woman he wanted her to be. The truth was that she couldn't afford a real phone with an expensive plan, but for emergencies, she kept one of those pay-as-you-go phones. Lately, however, she hadn't needed it. She was in yelling distance of the main part of town and she'd barely gone anywhere since Izzy was born. Yesterday the last of her minutes had run out.

"I am a responsible adult and I have things under control," she said. "All right?"

He didn't answer.

"Holt, I know what you do. People come to you with their problems and you fix them. I am not one of those people. I don't need you to fix my life. I just need you to help me with the clinic, but that's mostly for Larkville. I am off-limits," she said. "Is that clear?"

"Crystal," he said, his voice coming out clipped, but still as sexy as ever. "You're off-limits. That's a fine idea. I like it."

She had no idea what he meant by that, and since Holt hung up immediately afterward, she didn't have a chance to ask.

Not that he would have answered had she asked. Totally frustrating man. She was so glad that the two of them were only going to have to be together for a short time. It couldn't end fast enough for her. She wanted to be contented.

Not in a perpetual state of wondering what it would be like to kiss Holt again.

* * *

Holt woke up feeling edgy the morning that Kathryn was supposed to show up at the ranch. The doctor candidate from Chicago hadn't panned out and Holt had sent Kathryn an email to tell her so. He sent out more feelers, made more calls, asked for favors even though he hated doing that.

I can't wait for this to be over, he thought. All his life he had been the guy people turned to. And most of the time he was fine with that. There was a symbiotic relationship between the ranch and the locals, and he was a part of that.

People needed someone they could rely on, and for some reason a rancher seemed to fit their romantic vision of who that person should be. He'd learned to take all the requests in stride. He knew the rules, what to expect, how to play it.

But from the first, Kathryn had thrown him off his game. It was clear she had needs, that she could use some help. It was just as clear that, on a personal level, she didn't want to accept his help. What was a guy to do?

"Forget her," he told the nearest barnyard cat.

The cat seemed to give him the evil eye. Cats were good at that. Okay, he couldn't forget her yet. He had made promises. They had a job to do together. But what he needed to do was to stop thinking of her as a woman.

"Holt." A soft voice sounded behind him, and he pivoted. There she was, dressed in soft blue, a little bundle of baby strapped to her stomach in a cloth carrier. All he could see of the baby was Izzy's pale, fuzzy hair and her little arms and legs dangling from the carrier. Something stabbed at his heart. A mere leftover vestige of his time with Lilith. A reminder that this was not for him, not his path—that he couldn't handle it right, if at all. He looked into Kathryn's worried eyes.

"Ready?" he asked.

She gave a quick nod. "I was a little concerned when Nancy told me that you were away from the house."

He gave her a stern look. "You didn't trust me to stand by my word?"

"No," she said quickly. "It wasn't so much you. I just…I've grown used to being disappointed now and then."

He stared at her, knowing she was thinking

about her parents and ex-husband. "I'm not those people." He didn't bother explaining himself.

Kathryn stared straight into his eyes. "I'm sorry. Yes, I know."

"Whatever your parents and husband did to you—"

She shook her head. "It doesn't matter. I'm beyond it and it's no longer important. You're here. I'm here. We have work to do. If you're in, we're good to go."

Clearly, she was not "beyond it" if she'd worried that he might disappoint her, and trust was an issue, but she had finished up her sentence by flashing a big smile, and his breath had whooshed out of him. Already, her eyes were lighting up.

"And just where are we going?"

"I was thinking…I have an idea. Would you mind walking me around a bit of the ranch while we talk? I need to think—no, to *see*—if what I'm envisioning will work."

"It's just a ranch." He didn't want to think why he was so reluctant to show her the Double Bar C, even though he knew. Lilith had always had two complaints about him. One was that a ranch wasn't her style and that parts of it were dirty.

But Kathryn was giving him an odd, probing look.

"What?"

"This is your home, your livelihood, your everything, and all you can say is 'It's just a ranch.' You really are a man of few words."

And that had been Lilith's other complaint. He didn't have any intention of sharing his thoughts or his soul with her.

"Do you need a lot of words?"

She tilted her head, keeping one palm on the back of the baby's head, cuddling Izzy to her. Holt wished he hadn't noticed that.

"I like words," Kathryn finally said. "I like openness. But you and I don't have to be open. We're just business partners, so as long as you're still willing to help with the clinic, I can put up with your fear of communication."

He glowered at her; he might have even growled.

She raised one brow. And then she gave him an impish smile. "I still want to see the ranch."

"A ranch tour? You're on," he said. As he

turned to lead her away, their paths crossed and she bumped up against his side. His whole body began to hum, and he realized how much he'd been wanting to touch her. For days.

That was not good.

CHAPTER NINE

Sizzle, pop, ignore that touch. It was just an accident, a nothing touch. Belay all sensation, Kathryn ordered herself, but it wasn't an easy thing to do. With Holt, she was always a bit unbalanced. Half the time she struggled with her desire to kiss the man. The rest of the time she wanted to run as far from him as she could. He made her feel things she had no business feeling.

That was a concern. When she left here, she had to know she could be a world unto herself, not in need of another person's praise, affection, validation or financial support. Because needing people had always been her downfall.

That was why it was so difficult to accept the baby bounty that had come her way lately. Holt's half sister, Ellie Jackson, had dropped off a pretty outfit for Izzy, and she and Kathryn had bonded a bit. Kathryn was suddenly getting to know women she hadn't known her last time here.

Other anonymous gifts had simply appeared on her porch. The thought that Holt might be at the heart of all this wouldn't subside. The fact that he might be practicing his "ruler of the ranch" methods on her made her wary.

Still, even the most independent of people sometimes had to work *with* people to reach their goals.

"Why the sudden interest in ranching?" Holt asked in that sexy, grumpy way of his. She wished he didn't sound so…virile. Especially since she was still trying to forget what it had felt like when her body had come up against his in that accidental touch a moment ago.

Get your mind back on target, she ordered herself.

"Do you have places here where people could stay?" she asked, ignoring his grumpy question.

Those dark eyes were wary. "People? You?"

She felt the blush coming on and quickly turned away and tried to pretend that the horizon held some mystery for her. "Not me. Other people.

City people. People who might want to visit a ranch."

"This isn't a dude ranch."

"I know. I'm not suggesting you make it one."

"Good. Because this ranch doesn't just belong to me. There are a number of us Calhouns…and some other siblings, too, as you may have heard."

"How do you feel about your father's other children? You didn't even know they existed a few months ago."

He raised one brow.

There was that embarrassing blush again. "I don't mean to pry, or certainly to imply anything by that. I just— It has to be a shock to find out that you have half brothers and sisters."

"He wasn't married to my mother then, so it's none of my affair. I'm the keeper of the Calhoun ranch. If there are others, none of that changes my role."

Kathryn had a sudden urge to kiss Holt to see if she could get a reaction, to discover if there *were* real feelings lurking under that cool facade, but the heat that quickly rose in her at that thought told her that it would be a bad idea to kiss Holt.

Disastrous. He might be made of steel, but she was—unfortunately—human. And steel man or not, she was attracted to him.

She took a deep breath. "I promise not to hurt your ranch."

To her surprise, his lips tilted up in a hint of a smile. "I wasn't exactly worried about that."

"But you said—"

"I was just warning you about what I would and wouldn't allow. Hurting the ranch was never an option."

But she had heard that he might have hurt *women* before, broken their hearts, refused to give them what they wanted from him. That she could believe. Easily.

"Why are you asking me about housing people on the ranch?"

"I want to hold our fundraiser here. Just for a day, or a little more than a day."

"A fundraiser. Here? What kind of a fundraiser?"

"Not a big deal. Just a day at the Double Bar C. Let people see what really goes on at a ranch. Maybe let them get involved a bit. Not a real dude ranch experience, because this would just be for one day and possibly a night. And also because there would be other things going on, too."

He never dropped his gaze from her. She felt as if her clothes were too tight when she had already been doing her best to get back in shape.

"Kind of county fair-ish things," she volunteered without him asking. "Bake sales, animal competitions, maybe a rodeo."

"You want to turn the Double Bar C into a sideshow?"

"Maybe just a very *little* rodeo," she amended. "Because that's the kind of thing that people from the city, people with money, would pay to see. They get to play dress up and pretend they're cowboys for a day. City people like that. And if you show them some info on the clinic and what we're trying to do with their money, they'll like it even better. They might make donations. It always makes people feel good if they can do something good while tending to their own pleasures and fantasies."

That sexy eyebrow of his rose higher.

"Stop that," she said.

"Stop what?"

"Don't play innocent with me, Holt Calhoun. You may not be one for demonstrative displays, but you have a way of making a person feel as if she said something…wanton, when all she—*I*— was talking about was something perfectly innocent."

"If you keep using words like *pleasures* and *fantasies* and *wanton,* we're going to have trouble here." He wasn't smiling now.

And Kathryn *was* feeling rather wanton. Thank goodness she wasn't capable of *doing* anything wanton a little more than two weeks after having a baby. Otherwise, she might be embarrassing herself with Holt even more than she already was.

Needing to anchor and reassure herself, she shifted her hand over Izzy's soft, fuzzy head and the baby made that weak little moan that babies make.

As if he couldn't help himself, Holt's gaze flashed to Izzy and he looked away almost as if he'd been burned.

"I didn't have anywhere to leave her." Kathryn couldn't stop herself from saying the words. "I'm sorry. I know that being around her makes you uncomfortable."

"That's my problem, not hers." The intensity in his expression, the way he never flinched but stared a person straight in the eyes, made Kathryn want to take a step back. Trying to delve into the soul of a man like Holt…what would a woman find?

Heat, she thought. *Power. Passion that had been leashed for a long time.*

A choking sound rose up in Kathryn's throat. "Excuse me," she said. "I need to—to get Izzy out of the sun. I'll be back." She rushed off toward the ranch house, feeling like a coward, but she didn't like the direction her thoughts had turned. Holt seemed to have that effect on her every time they met. Still. She hated the fact that she couldn't seem to control herself around him.

Run, her senses told her.

"Don't you dare," she whispered to herself. "No." She took a deep breath and entered the house.

Nancy was in the kitchen. She looked at Kathryn,

studied her for a second. "Did you and Holt fight?"

Kathryn blinked. "No. I just… Holt…"

"Yes," Nancy said. "He's a good man, but not an easy one. Are you leaving?"

It sounded a lot as if Nancy thought that Holt had run Kathryn off. Kathryn quickly shook her head. "No. We have plans to make, but—" she looked down at Izzy and issued a silent apology, feeling as if she was getting in the bad habit of using her child as an excuse much the way her parents had used her "—is there a place I can put Izzy down? I have her baby carrier with me."

"A baby carrier?" Nancy said. "I can do better than that. Come on, sweetie. May I?" she asked Kathryn, holding out her arms.

Kathryn handed over her child. "Are you sure?"

Nancy cuddled the baby close. "We don't get ones this little around here. Brady isn't really a baby anymore. I'm going to enjoy this time. You just go take care of whatever business you and Holt have."

"Thank you," Kathryn said. She could see that Nancy would lay her life down for a child, but it was still difficult to leave Izzy. She dropped a kiss on Izzy's head and turned to go.

"Kathryn?"

"Yes?" she said, turning back slightly.

"I know he's a harsh man in some ways, but a man like Holt, who holds everything inside, doesn't forget or forgive easily. Lilith lived in Larkville when they were engaged. There were rumors that she was pregnant and that he had to find out about that from someone else. There was more, but I don't know how much of it was made up and how much was true. Holt never said, but the way he feels about babies, I think there's a good chance that there was a baby involved. We'll probably never know. He's not a man who opens up. But he's a good man."

There it was. Again.

"I know that," Kathryn said. And she did. She also knew that Holt was a powerful man. Too powerful for someone like her. And now she knew for sure that he had major baby issues. All those were good things to remember. "Thank you again," she told Nancy.

She went outside to find Holt. He was on a ladteen days. He and I are just getting started and he's not real happy, but it's necessary. In a very short time, he's gonna come running for the bottle, no coaxing needed."

"I feel kind of dumb, having lived here but knowing so little about raising cattle."

"We all know what we need to know, I guess. You never had any need to know cattle." And he had never needed to know anything about raising babies. "Where's the baby?" he asked, as if he just couldn't help it. He frowned.

"Don't worry. I don't have her hidden on my body somewhere. Nancy's got her. Now that she's a few weeks old, they're communicating."

"Nancy likes babies." Holt wanted to swear. Everything he said seemed to shout, *I don't like babies!* Which wasn't true. He just hadn't gotten over losing his. He still wanted his child. Maybe someday he'd get his act together, learn how to treat a baby right and have one of his own, but this one was spoken for. She wasn't going to stay, and he couldn't bear the loss of another baby. It was better not to get attached to things you had to give up. "You came about my questions?" he asked, trying to change the subject and forget about the unchangeable past.

"I came to tell you that I never expected you to do so much. I wouldn't have approached you at all if I'd had any connections to people who could help provide a doctor or if I had the kind of pull you do with the people of Larkville."

Holt scowled. "Has anyone here been treating you wrong?"

"Not at all. In fact, I've been gifted with their largesse. Baby items keep appearing on my porch, and I've made friends I never had when I lived here before. I'm grateful, especially since people don't really have any reason at all to be so darned sweet to me. I pretty much drifted through my teen years here without connecting."

"Not your fault. You told me your parents kept you apart from the rest of the town."

"Any ordinary teen would have rebelled."

He couldn't help chuckling.

"What?"

"You sounded downright irritated that you by-passed the rebellious teen phase."

"Did you? Rebel, I mean?"

He had tried to. "I did a few things. Raised some hell. Busted up a car or two. Got drunk." Got a woman pregnant. But by then he'd left his teen years behind. It still galled him that he had messed up that way on so many levels. "Mostly, though, I had to walk the straight and narrow. If you don't take care of your animals, well, ranching can be life or death. You have to time your hell-raising right or everyone suffers."

She laughed at that, and her laugh was soft, musical, enticing. He growled.

"Don't growl at me," she said, surprising him.

"I wasn't."

"You were looking at me when you growled."

He wondered if her jerk of a husband had done stuff like that. "Why'd you marry a guy like that, anyway?"

She blushed, her cheeks turning a pretty rose as she looked to the side. "When I was growing up and things were so bad, I couldn't wait to get away and be on my own. I floated along for a while just enjoying college and my studies, but when I met James, well, he could be charming and complimentary. And when we got married, he was in grad school and I gave up my own plans in order to take any job I could get to support us. But when I started communicating with one of my former professors who suggested I might want to attend grad school myself when James finished, things got really ugly. James was jealous, he needed adoration, and when I got pregnant…well, I learned a lot about men who need to be in control. They don't like having that control taken from them. My own fault for not seeing it sooner."

"Some men hide things well." It was a warning. To her. To him.

"Well, now I have better and more effective armor than I used to." She met his challenge.

"Do you now?" He looked at her the way a man looks at a woman he wants, and her blush deepened, but she didn't look away.

"You can't scare me into thinking that you're bad, you know," she said. "You're…you're ornery at times, and we want different things from life, but I see what you do. You pretend to be mean, but you're not mean. In fact, you're rather a soft touch."

And she was digging into areas he didn't want anyone to go. "What are you here for really, Kathryn? I've got work to do."

She blew out a breath. "I don't even want to admit it, but you asked me some questions I don't know the answers to. So I'm here to find out the answers."

"Excuse me?"

"You help show me what goes on at the ranch and then I'll tell you what events I want to have. And I'm not letting you do all the work, either," she said. "Thanks to you, I'm getting to know a whole lot more people in the town and I know how to get them to help out. I just need to decide what will work best. I'll make some choices and run them by you. Will you… Can you find some time during this week to show me around? What would be good for you?"

Never would be good for him. He liked looking at her and touching her and just listening to her talk far too much. And she had that cute little baby…

He made his mind go blank for a second.

"I can show you around today." Best to get this over with.

She looked at the calf who had finished the bottle. "What happened to having work to do and ranching being life or death?"

"I do, and it is. But I run the ranch now. I hire good people and I have a crew of hands I can call on to moonlight for me when I need to."

"Okay. Just let me go check in on Izzy and talk to Nancy."

He started to tell her that he would just call Nancy on his phone, but he thought she might need to do some "momma" things like feed the baby, things he didn't want to think about. And this would give him time to come up with a plan for the tour.

Instead, he walked her up to the house. Moving beside her, watching the sun catch the lighter streaks in her wheat hair, he breathed in her scent, and his body reacted instantly. That he could ignore…mostly. But when she turned to go inside, she gave him a brilliant smile. "I know showing off your ranch to city girls probably isn't high on your list of things you want to do, but I trust you not to go easy on me."

"Wouldn't dream of it."

She nodded. Then her smile faded a bit and she got a serious, anxious look in her eyes. "Holt, I have a job interview."

Which meant she might be leaving soon. He tried to ignore the punch to his gut. "That's great. Congratulations."

"Thank you, but it does mean that I need to do as much as I can for the clinic quickly. I don't want to leave this job half-finished. That wouldn't be right."

He started to tell her that he would finish it for her, even though the thought of going on without her made him feel oddly empty, but as he opened his mouth, she spoke.

"In spite of my degree, I've never done any-thing of this magnitude before and I need to do it right. I—I have something to prove to myself."

"Understood. But even the rancher needs help. Everyone does."

She studied him as if he had just lied to her.

"Says the man who doesn't like to ask people for help."

"I have employees."

"Exactly. They're *employees*. You pay them. They're not doing you a favor."

He gave her the evil eye he had perfected.

She laughed and reached up and patted his cheek. "Just be aware that I may be running full tilt until this is done. While I'm forced to ask people to help with some things, I want to do as much as I can on my own."

"You'll make yourself sick."

She smiled and turned away. "No. But I'll do something important. I'll help people and make a difference. I'll secure my future. I hope."

What was a guy supposed to say to that? "Go talk to Nancy and do what you need to do with Izzy. I'll give you the whirlwind tour when you're done."

A bark had Kathryn turning to greet Blue, who was bearing down on her like a fast-moving tank. She dropped to her knees, which made the dog even taller than she was. Then she gave the evil-looking mutt a big hug. Blue's teeth could take a chunk out of her if he was so inclined. Holt knew that he wouldn't, but Kathryn couldn't know that. She'd only met the dog once.

"Hi, sweetie," she said, receiving a slobbery lick for her troubles.

Holt gave her a look. *Too innocent,* he wanted to say. If this didn't end soon, she would surely make him crazy.

"What?" she asked, a challenge in her eyes.

He started to tell her that nothing was wrong. Instead, he faced her head-on. "I've seen men run when Blue comes at them, but you didn't, not even that first time."

She shrugged. "I guess I figured that even if you wanted me gone, you still wouldn't let your dog eat me."

He didn't say anything.

"I know you think that I'm a bit naive, but I'm not. Not anymore. To prove it, here are the people in town who've won my respect and friendship." She rattled off a small group which concluded with Jess, Nancy and himself. "These are the people I don't know well enough to decide about yet," she said, giving him another list. "And these are the people who make me uncomfortable." There were only two people on that list, both of them bad. Then she raised one delicate, sexy brow. "Am I wrong?"

"I'm thinking about it." But her laughter rang out behind him as he walked away, and he couldn't help but smile. Not that she would know it. His back was to her. He, however, knew one thing. Kathryn Ellis kept him on his toes. And when she challenged him she made him hot. Oh, yes, risky as it was, he was definitely going to kiss her again before she left.

CHAPTER TWELVE

"I NEVER knew this ranch was this big," Kathryn said as Holt drove her around the perimeter and then down some of the interior roads.

"Needs to be. Cattle need a lot of land, a lot of grass."

"And you have horses, too."

"Yes. Enough to do the jobs that can't be done from a truck."

"When can't you use a truck?"

"If you're trying to catch a runaway cow, the truck can go faster than a horse, but it doesn't maneuver nearly as well and there are places it just can't go. Driving a truck, you can't cut back and change directions quickly enough to stay with a cow that doesn't want to get caught. And a horse, once the cow is caught, is more sensitive to the movements of the animal than a truck driver can be. An ATV will do the job, but ATVs, like trucks, can stress the cows more than a horse will. Besides, a lot of cowmen just like horses. We like them on a personal basis, we like the history of them, we don't want them disappearing from the ranch, so there are days, at least on the Double Bar C, when we take out the horses just because it's the right thing to do. A prized truck is great, but a prized horse and a cowboy…that's an unbreakable bond."

"Is that how you feel about Daedalus?"

"He's special," Holt agreed, restraining his praise. He didn't want to get sappy in front of Kathryn. The woman saw way too much.

"I assume you'll be okay with people riding your horses at the fundraiser?"

"I thought that was a given."

"Good. Because I'd like to ride Daedalus. I've never really ridden a horse before."

He stopped the truck. "You're kidding, right? I know what you said about being a city girl and not taking part in Larkville society, but this is Texas, Kathryn. Ranch country. That's practically criminal." He turned the truck toward home.

She saw where he was headed. "Did I make you angry?"

"Yes."

Kathryn sighed.

"What?"

"That's your only response?"

"You asked a question. I answered it."

"You're angry with me because I haven't ridden a horse before?"

"I'm angry that no one, including me, knew that." He pulled the truck up in the drive. "Come on," he said, surprising her by taking her hand again.

Her palm slid against his. She tried not to savor the sensation of touching Holt too much, but this had been one of her teenage fantasies—Holt holding her hand. It felt as good as she had imagined it would, as good as it had the last time they'd touched. And now things got worse. She felt hot. Shivery. All this just from Holt's hand wrapped around hers. What would she do if he wrapped his arms around her and kissed her again?

Idiot. Stop it, she told herself as she tried to turn her attention back to more practical matters.

Neither did she ask where they were going. It was obvious. Or so she thought. When they got to the barn, he went into what she guessed was a tack room and started looking around. "These will have to do," he finally said, giving her a pair of boots that were, she guessed, about a size too big. "These were my mother's, but as long as you can keep them on, they'll be better than nothing."

Kathryn sat right down and put the boots on. She was going to ride a horse. Holt was going to show her how. She grinned at him. He smiled back, just a little. Her heart flipped around.

Easy, she told herself. *Don't react.* But the man was just too potent. She could see why Lilith had been upset that he couldn't open his heart to her. A woman would do a lot to get a man like this to say the words she wanted to hear. None of that excused the heinous things Holt's ex-fiancée had done. But it made Kathryn understand a little. And it made her very wary.

"You've been wanting to do this a long time, haven't you?" he asked.

"I never thought about it too much, but now that

I am, I love anything that broadens my horizons. When you spend your childhood and marriage in a vacuum, every new experience is exciting."

Great. A ranch was, for all its acres, a pretty small microcosm. As Lilith had told him repeatedly, she craved the world. Fashion. Excitement. The theater. Anything that wasn't a ranch. Soon enough Kathryn would have tried all there was to try on a ranch. And then?

Then she'd do what she'd planned all along and head off to her new job that could only be done in a city.

Holt saddled and mounted Daedalus. Then he motioned Kathryn over to the fence and held out his hand to her.

She looked at his hand as if it was a rattlesnake. "I thought you were going to teach me to ride, not treat me like a baby."

"Learning to do anything requires baby steps," he said. "You want to ride Daedalus, but he's too much of a handful for a beginner." Still, he knew that part of the reason he was doing this was because he wanted Kathryn behind him, her arms around his waist. And he wanted—for a few minutes, anyway—to stop waiting for her smile, which would be simple if he couldn't see her face. The truth was that he was feeling seriously besotted. That was bad.

In seconds, she had swung up behind him. He groaned inwardly as her hands circled his waist and she nudged up against him, her soft breasts against his back.

"Now we'll take a slow ride until you get used to the motion," he said, trying to keep his voice from going thick.

"Okay." Her voice was a bit whispery. He knew she wasn't immune to him. She had gotten into that kiss the other day with fervor. He was insane for torturing them both this way.

"Let's—let's figure out which things we'll do on the cowboy day," she suggested.

"Good idea." Anything to take his mind off his very bad idea of having Kathryn riding behind him. Together they decided on a few events. Riding, of course. A little roping. Teaching riders to dally and tie on, which he had to explain to her were two methods of securing a rope to a saddle once you'd caught your cow.

"Cowboys tend to be passionate about their favorite method," he told her. "Some parts of the country favor one or the other. Here at the Double Bar C, we use the one that fits the situation. Is that enough events for the day?"

"Not quite. How about some fence mending?" she suggested. "And helping with that bridge you said you were going to repair."

"I'm going to fix the bridge before the guests show up."

"No. People will like it better if they know they're doing a real job, not a made-up one. And since I talked you into this, it's only right that you should get something back."

He had already gotten something back. He was pretty sure that just getting to know Kathryn was going to be the highlight of his days when he thought back on this summer.

They agreed on a few more events for those who were less inclined to the ranching side of things: baking and jam contests, lessons in soap making and other artisan crafts that Holt knew some of the ranchers' wives excelled at. And, of course, the minirodeo at the end of the day, followed by fireworks. But when Daedalus shied slightly at a bee and Kathryn tightened her hold on him, bumping up against him, Holt decided to put an end to this exquisite torture.

"Now alone," he said, switching things around so that he was on the ground and Kathryn was riding single. He led Daedalus around and showed Kathryn how to command the horse to do as she wished.

"I never knew how much fun this could be," she said with a smile. "I wonder if fence mending will be as much fun."

Despite himself, he chuckled "You actually sound as if you're looking forward to mending fences. Think of the unpleasant jobs I could have talked you into if I'd only known."

"Your loss. Too late now," she teased as she made another loop around the corral.

Eventually, though, the time came for her to get down. Holt held up his arms and she went into them. It was all he could do not to slide her down his body, but that trusting look in her eyes did him in. He had to behave, even though it was killing him.

Her feet had barely touched the ground, however, when she rose on her toes and kissed him on the cheek. Just one kiss. Feather-soft. Sweet. Nothing sensual about it. But it was torture. Not touching her was torture. But so very necessary. He was starting to lose control around her, and wasn't that one of Kathryn's concerns? She wanted to be in control.

"I hope you get that job you're in line for," he said as she put Izzy in her car. He meant it. If he spent too much longer with Kathryn, he was going to do something that was going to leave both of them filled with regret for a very long time. Even after she was gone.

Holt tried to put his head down and just work during the next couple of weeks. The fundraiser was scheduled three weeks from now and there was a lot to do to get the ranch in shape to receive visitors. He'd been in touch with friends and business associates in Texas, Illinois and New York, sending out as big a net as he could in the hopes of tempting one qualified doctor to tiny Larkville. All of that had to be scheduled around the regular ranch duties.

Not that he was complaining about the work. Anything he could do to keep from thinking about Kathryn with her hands on him or Kathryn with her lips on him or just Kathryn was fine by him. There was something about the woman that just drove him mad, and he was pretty sure he knew what it was. During the time he had been taking care of Hank and since then, he had been without any intimate female companionship. Unfortunately, right now there was no other woman that he was attracted to even if he'd had time. But just as soon as all this clinic stuff was over and Kathryn and her baby were back where they belonged, he was going to have to do something about that. As it was, he was half-afraid he was going to grab her and kiss her—or worse—in public, and that wouldn't be good for either of them.

But while he was waiting, he was going to stay away and keep his mind off her as much as possible. At least that was the plan.

Unfortunately, it was difficult to stick to. When

he went to town for supplies a few days later, he kept wondering whether Kathryn was at the doctor's office, the newspaper or at home, and how she was managing with the baby. Quickly, he tried to kick those thoughts from his mind.

"Hey, Holt," Gus said when he stopped at Gus's Fillin' Station. "I hear that pretty little gal of yours is creating quite a stir in the town. Got everybody buzzin' and doin'."

Holt's brain had frozen on the words *that pretty little gal of yours*. "You're talking about Kathryn?"

"Who else? I've never seen anybody go at anything with such fire. It sounds like a mountain of a job, but she's always got a smile on her face. She smiles even while she's askin' you to do something, and before you know it, you're saying yes and likin' it, too."

"What exactly is she asking?"

"Oh, you know, would I dress up like a cowboy in full gear for that cowboy thing she's so excited about. And how much will it cost for me to fix her car so it won't break down on the way to the ranch. And will I drive the bus she's borrowing from the school district to bus any of the visitors who need bussing, because she knows she can trust me to get them there safe. And then, besides paying me to fix her car, she promised me cookies and kissed me on the cheek when I said yes, I would dress up and drive the bus."

"She did, huh?" Holt couldn't help sounding grumpy. Or grumpier than usual. Even though it was dumb as hell to be jealous of Kathryn kissing Gus on the cheek. Gus was an old man...but he was a nice man. He had been on Kathryn's list of people she liked. And age might not matter to Kathryn. It certainly wouldn't matter to Gus...or any man for that matter. Kathryn was too damn pretty and she had that smile that made a man feel as if he might burst into flame without any fuel.

He almost growled, forgetting himself. Then he shook himself. Stupid. Gus was his friend, and Kathryn was an exuberant woman. Just because some people—like himself—were shallow and emotionally stunted didn't mean that everyone else was.

"Hey, Holt," Gus said as Holt started to leave.

He turned and saw Gus rubbing his neck and frowning the way people did when they were about to broach an uncomfortable subject. Holt quickly considered all the possibilities. Could be a money question. Was the station in financial trouble? Could be an animal question, but that wouldn't make Gus uncomfortable and—

"Hey, Holt, I...uh, I was reading a book on the history of Texas the other day. Thought you might like to borrow it."

Holt blinked. What the— A book? "Sure, Gus. That'd be real nice. Thanks."

Gus scowled. He looked incredibly relieved.

As Holt went on his way, he wondered what that had been about. He and Gus had never had an exchange like that before. They'd never even discussed books or history. Mostly they talked about cars and guns. Maybe horses. But as Holt went about his business in town, a pattern quickly developed. Almost everyone he ran into that day offered him something: cookies, pickles, jam; Mrs. Best brought him a framed photograph of his daddy from when she and Clay were young. And everyone he met—after they had gotten past this awkward gifting stage—had some tale to tell him about how Kathryn had them eager to help her out. The town was a whole lot more excited about Kathryn's cowboy day than they even were about football. That said a lot about the woman. And judging by the talk he'd heard, it sounded as if she was running herself ragged.

Maybe he would stop by her place for a minute—just to make sure she didn't have any color-coded lists she needed to send him. No point in her emailing him if he was here in the flesh, was there? It would save her some trouble.

Unfortunately, his plan wasn't as simple as it sounded. For a town this small, Kathryn really seemed to get around. She wasn't at home, at work or at the SmartMart. He didn't see her at Hal's Drug and Photo, either. And he knew she wouldn't be in the Saddle Up Bar or the Cattleman's Association Hall. By the time he got to the town hall and ran into the mayor, Holt was starting to get worried. "Kathryn?" he asked tersely.

Fortunately, Johanna was used to his ways, and being a woman who knew how to cut to the chase, she simply told him what he wanted. "At the park."

"Thanks."

She moved toward him.

"You're not going to give me anything, are you?" he asked.

The poised, middle-aged, never nonplussed mayor actually looked a bit discomfited. "A bottle of wine?" she suggested.

"Kathryn?" he asked.

"Don't be upset with her. She was just trying to give back, not make you feel uncomfortable." She handed him the wine. He thanked her, somewhat awkwardly.

"Don't worry. I won't make her pay for my embarrassment. Much." He headed out again.

Johanna cleared her throat and he waited. "She's with Izzy." The fact that she even felt compelled to mention it—did everyone in town know that he wasn't good around babies? Had Kathryn told them? He didn't think she would. But he put his head down and set off to find her, wondering what he would say to her when he found her. Telling himself to slap some self-control on before he did something stupid. Like back her up against a tree and mold his body to hers.

Just before he read her the riot act for making people think—for some weird reason—that they needed to give him Christmas presents in the summer.

Put a rein on it, Calhoun, he ordered himself and he thought he was doing pretty well. When he arrived at the park, he came upon an idyllic scene. The grass was green, the sun was shining, the baby was asleep on a blanket in the shade of a tree and Kathryn sat beside her, her blond head bent over a batch of papers on her lap. Holt tried not to notice just how small and innocent Izzy looked. Instead, he turned his attention to Katherine as he moved toward her. His steps were silent on the grass, and he was already standing next to the blanket by the time she noticed him there.

For half a second he thought he saw something in her eyes that made him feel overly warm, but that was probably just his imagination. Maybe just his own wishful thinking because it was gone as soon as it had appeared. She smiled at him.

"You caught me goofing off," she said, her voice low to keep from waking the baby.

He sank to one knee beside her and touched the edge of her papers with one finger. "Do you even know how to goof off? Looks like more lists."

"Some of them are, but my mind was wandering when you showed up. That counts as goofing off."

"Doesn't exactly sound like fun."

"How do you know? In my mind I was in a dreamworld."

He raised one brow. "Doing what? With whom?"

Oh, now he had made her blush. Maybe he had been trying to. She was amazingly pretty when she blushed, and today, tipping her head back, she looked like a woman waiting to be kissed. Or a woman planning on kissing a man. Either way, she looked too damned enticing.

"Nothing like that," she said. "It wasn't that kind of dream. There wasn't a man involved."

Good. "So it was a fun dream, but there was no man involved."

"Exactly. I was practicing affirmative thinking."

"I see." He didn't. "And what were you affirming?"

"I was…it's silly, but I was imagining myself in my own apartment, somewhere in a city. I've just been asked to oversee the redevelopment of an aging part of town, one that needs revitalizing. The people who've hired me know I can do it, because I get results. And what that means is…"

"Lots of money?"

She shook her head. "No. Well, maybe. It means that I can give Izzy all that she needs. I can protect her." Kathryn's voice was quiet but intense. Clearly this was something she worried about. It was the thing that woke her up at night.

Holt's mind went dark. He tried not to think about how alone in the world Kathryn was. He didn't have the right to go there. He didn't even know how to express the confusing, conflicting sensations that were flitting through him. "Good things will happen for you," he said. "Have to. They wouldn't dare elude you. You're a fighter."

"It wasn't all selfish stuff I was thinking about,

either," she said as if wanting to protect your kid was even close to selfish. But he knew what she meant. The apartment. The job and accolades. "I was imagining Ava DuShay calling me. She's the lady who's most worried about Dr. Cooper leaving. She was telling me that she loved the new doctor and the clinic and that now she wouldn't have to worry about her son coming back to Larkville and putting her in a home."

"Mrs. DuShay worries about that?"

"Yes. Her son lives—"

"In Dallas. Yes, I know Buddy. He's an ass. A bigger ass than I am."

"Well, I know you wouldn't be putting her in a home if she was your concern."

"Damn straight I wouldn't." He frowned.

"I probably shouldn't have mentioned that," she said. "You're looking fierce."

"I'm thinking that I need to talk to Buddy when he comes to town next time. Maybe move his nose to one side of his face. Making his momma worry like that."

"I think she might worry more if you punched

Buddy. He's her son, and she loves him no matter what. You can understand that, can't you?"

He stared at her. She knew darn well he wasn't a sensitive guy. He didn't *want* to be a sensitive guy. He didn't want to *feel*. Feelings brought trouble and everything bad that had ever happened to him had been a result of out-of-control emotions.

"Anyway, she isn't going to have to worry about that," he said, ignoring his thoughts. "We'll get a doctor. You'll get that phone call. And you'll get that job, too. Anyone can see that you know how to get things done. I must have met twenty people today telling me about what they were doing for their part of the fundraiser."

"Yes, they're excited, aren't they?" she asked. "*I'm* excited, too. This is going to be so much fun! Everyone's going to have a great time. I talked to Nan and she says that the Bunk'n'Grill is booked solid. I asked her to see if she could find some more places to put people. Nan's on it."

He smiled in spite of himself.

"What?"

"Did you promise her cookies?"

She looked guilty. "I promised I'd teach her to

braid beads in her hair. She likes quirky things like that. But she would have done it without. Nan doesn't need bribing. No one here does. I just— They're all working so hard, I want them to know I appreciate it."

"You're not even going to benefit from the clinic."

"You know I will. I'll get to talk about it in job interviews and, more than that, I'll just know I helped make it happen. My point is, people are capable of doing a lot of things they might not think they're capable of doing if they don't have you to run to. I'll bet they all got along when you were out of town."

"So you *are* the elf?"

"Excuse me?" Oh, weren't those gray eyes pretty when she opened them that wide?

"You know what I mean, Kathryn," he said, his voice low. "I have a pickup truck full of food and other gifts. What's that all about?"

"People always take their problems to you. They…love you, just like they did your father. I just thought maybe they might not have thought about how much work taking care of them is and that they might, maybe, possibly, want to show you that they appreciate you in some way other than simply saying how great you are. Speaking of which…" She turned to rummage in her bag.

He saw what she was going to do and automatically, without thinking, he put his hand over hers. He tried to ignore the softness of her skin and how his own flesh reacted to this simple touch. Kathryn froze and turned to him.

"Not you," he said, his voice tight. "You've been doing all the work. You don't get to do the payback thing."

"You saved me and Izzy. I never paid you back for that."

"Sure you did."

"How?"

But he got stubborn. *You lived. You're safe,* he thought. That was her payback to him. But he would never say that. That was delving into territory he didn't want to and wouldn't traverse. Especially now.

"I'll let you give me some of Gus's cookies."

"How do you know I wasn't going to give you cookies?"

He chuckled then. "I guess I don't. Just don't give me anything. I don't want payback."

She crossed her arms. "Are you going to tell me that you turned all those people down?"

He frowned. "No. I didn't. I wanted to, but I didn't. It would have created problems."

"It would have hurt their feelings."

"Yes."

She smiled. Brilliantly.

"What?"

"You turned down my gift. That means you consider me an equal, a partner, because you didn't worry about hurting my feelings."

"You have too much sense to take anything I say or do to heart. We've discussed this before."

"You're darn right. You and I are…friends. We don't have to stand on ceremony." Suddenly she gave him a strange look. She had risen to her knees and crossed her arms. There was a stern look in those gorgeous gray eyes. Kathryn looked at his pocket. "I see you have another of those little scraps of paper, those *lists,*" she emphasized. "Who asked you to do what today?"

Holt felt like a kid who had gotten caught passing notes at school. He was half tempted to cover his pocket with his hand. "There's not much on it."

"And you say that you don't make lists…" she drawled.

"Your lists would make my lists ashamed to be called lists." He pulled the slip of paper from his pocket. "Not a single color code in sight and only two items on it."

She took a look. "These are both things they could figure out on their own. Not that I can talk. I've asked you to do more for me than anyone else has. Thank goodness that, as I told you, I'm done asking you for things."

"I know what you said. You're telling me I'm expendable." For some reason, that ticked him off. All his life he'd been following in his father's footsteps, being everyone's go-to guy and—yes—he seldom admitted it even to himself, but there *had* been times when he'd wished he could step out from under the weight of all that responsibility for a while. But now? Here with Kathryn telling him she didn't want his help?

She looked totally surprised. "I've…offended you?"

"No. I'm not offended." He was…he didn't know what in hell he was.

"I just wanted you to know that I realized I shouldn't have pushed you so hard. You made the calls, you gave me your ranch to more or less destroy, you lent me Nancy when I needed her, you gave up your time, you even gave me riding lessons and you made sure Izzy was born safely. I came back to Larkville determined to declare my independence and make it on my own. Asking you for so much…I took too much help from you. I should have stood on my own feet more."

"Who told you that?"

She was shaking her head, looking sad and lovely. "I didn't need to be told. Growing up, I was powerless, but when I married…I take credit for making that mistake. James might have been a controlling man, but I was the one who married him and allowed that to happen to myself. That's why I have to be my own person and be much more proactive."

"You *are*."

"Good. I can't be that woman again. When I got pregnant with Izzy—I had been sick and I neglected to take a couple of my birth control pills—James flew into a rage. He didn't want her. That's when I knew I had to leave him and I had to change. So immediately asking you to help me was not the way to go."

He shook his head.

"What?"

He was as angry as any man could be inside. At himself. At her stupid ex-husband. At any man who made a woman feel guilty for not agreeing to be under his thumb. But he smiled. "If you think you seemed dependent when you asked for my help, you're wrong. You were persistent. Stubborn. Annoying."

"I was scared."

"Could have fooled me. You were bold. A dog that wasn't going to let go of a bone. You were ready to fight me for what you wanted, to make it clear that I was being a stubborn idiot. And you were right. I had the contacts. This is my town, these are my people, they're my responsibility.

And you wouldn't take no. That's not being dependent, and you know it."

She blew out a breath. "I know it. And I'm proud that I was able to walk away from James and of my part in trying to make this clinic happen. But that still doesn't make it right that I and every person in town over the age of eighteen comes to you to solve all their problems. That has just got to stop."

"No."

"Holt…"

He gave her a "don't go there" look.

She grumbled something under her breath.

"What?"

"I said that you're a damned stubborn man."

"That I am. Deal with it, hon."

"You can't tell me you're always fine with everyone leaning on you. You fought me tooth and nail."

"Because you asked me to do the asking. I sure as hell don't like that." But she was right. There were days when he wanted to feel free to say, "I don't have time today." So why was he arguing so hard? He knew why. Because if he admitted it, she would stop asking him for things. And then he'd have no reason for these intimate little conversations.

His blood ran hot thinking of the word *intimate*. His blood ran cold thinking of ending his time with her.

"I know you don't like asking," she agreed, and she looked up at him. Suddenly he wasn't thinking about her ex-husband or the clinic or the town. He was thinking about *not* asking. Just doing exactly what he wanted to do.

Holt reached out and slid his hand beneath her hair. He cupped her neck, drew her closer. Now they were body to body, her breasts to his chest, her thighs against his, and he was staring down into her eyes. Then his lips were on hers, on all that berry softness, feeling the pressure of her mouth as she returned his kiss and made him burn. He pressed closer, took more. Any second now he was going to slide his palm down her curves, take as much of her as he possibly could. Right here in a public place.

"Hell." The single word came out too loud.

Then he heard a small sound, just the slightest

of sounds, a tiny whimpering. He froze. Kathryn practically leaped away from him. Izzy was stirring. The baby who ruled Kathryn's world, her reason for living, her reason for most of what she did. Soon it would just be Kathryn and Izzy.

Holt withdrew his hand and moved away.

Kathryn sat down on her heels. "I'm sorry," she said.

"For what?" he asked as nonchalantly as he could given the fact that his body was still aching for her.

"Don't do that."

He didn't pretend to misunderstand. "You think I'm going to blame you for not wanting to roll around on the ground with your baby right there?"

"Some men would." He could imagine who she was talking about. He wanted to tell her that he wouldn't be like that. He wanted to make her promises. How idiotic was that? It wasn't going to happen.

Instead, he reached into his pocket and pulled out a slip of paper.

"I don't understand." She took it as he rose and started to walk away.

"It's a list of three potential doctor candidates," he told her. "They'll all be here at the fundraiser."

And then he took off. Fast. Giving her the list of candidates was, after all, what he'd really come to do, anyway, wasn't it? He surely hadn't come to tell Kathryn that she made him crazy, that he found himself remembering her behind him on that horse, that he thought of touching her all the time.

He definitely hadn't come here to kiss her.

CHAPTER THIRTEEN

HOLT wasn't even out of the park when Kathryn's cell phone rang. She answered it, hung up, grabbed Izzy and started running. She must have been making a fuss because Holt turned around.

"Kathryn, what's wrong?"

"Nothing. Everything. That was the town of Skyridge, Illinois, calling. The city manager has been called out of town and he wants to push the video interview to now rather than two days from now. I have to get home, change clothes, set up the computer with the camera and…and…" She looked at Izzy. "I have to get Izzy to Johanna or Gracie or Mrs. Best. Fast. What if Izzy started squealing or crying while I was in the middle of the interview? I hate dropping her off on someone or feeling like I'm getting rid of her, but—"

"Give her here," Holt said, and he held out his arms.

Kathryn stopped babbling. She stared at him.

He glared at her. "Don't say anything. Don't argue. You don't have time to talk about it. I won't hurt her."

"I'll try to make it short," she said, reluctantly giving Izzy over to him.

"Make it what it has to be. This is your moment. Now go. Call me when you want her back."

She leaned forward, kissed Izzy, said, "I love you, baby," and then sprinted toward her house. She tried not to think about how Holt had avoided all things Izzy up until now. She was 100 percent certain he wouldn't let anything harm the baby, but she wasn't so sure about Izzy's effect on him. This was a man who had known he had a child on the way and had had that child taken from him forever.

The stress of worrying about what was going on between Holt and Izzy made Kathryn's smile too tense, her answers falsely bright. Her mind wasn't on the interview and she was faking it. Ed Austen, the interviewer, had a million questions, but he seemed particularly interested in the clinic and the "Come Be a Cowboy Day." "Sounds like a winner," he said.

"I hope so," Kathryn said, her mind still wandering to Izzy and Holt. Then she realized what she was saying, what she was doing—or not doing—and she sat up straighter, looking directly toward the screen. This was her baby's future. She couldn't waste it. Worrying wouldn't change what was going on with Holt and Izzy. "We're at capacity right now," she said, sitting up straighter, "and everyone is ready. This fundraiser should give us a good start on beginning our work on the clinic."

"And what if you leave? Who will make it happen then?"

Kathryn didn't even hesitate. "Holt Calhoun, Johanna Hollis, the mayor." She rattled off the names of several other people. "Almost everyone in the town, really. They've all gotten into the spirit of things. But Holt's the one who's helped the most. He'll follow through." She owed him for that. She hoped he had found someone at Gracie's or Johanna's to babysit Izzy. As soon as she had the thought, she was sure that he had. Holt got things done. He would find a capable sitter.

Kathryn breathed a sigh of relief and settled in to give the best interview she could. But the second it was over, she didn't even bother to change back into her more casual clothes. Instead, she bolted out the door and headed straight for the mayor's office.

"Holt? Izzy?" she asked Johanna when she didn't see either him or Izzy.

"Not a clue," Johanna said. "Is there a problem?"

"Oh…no." *Maybe*. Kathryn started to head toward Gracie May's Diner when she remembered what had almost flown past her in her haste to get to the interview. Holt had told her to call. She did that now and realized that she could hear his phone ringing. He was still in the park not fifty yards away. He had his back up against a tree; he was holding Izzy up and making raspberries on her little belly.

Kathryn's heart stopped. Her brain stopped. Her mouth…maybe it fell open. She wasn't thinking about herself that much. What she *did* think

about was how Izzy was laughing and clutch-
ing great fistfuls of Holt's hair. And pulling. Her
hands might be tiny, but Kathryn knew how hard
they could clutch at things. That had to hurt.

The strangest thing was that though Holt was
clearly amusing Izzy, he was holding her as if
she were a piece of delicate glass. And he wasn't
laughing back. He wasn't reacting.

Until Izzy, in her excitement, spit up all over
his shirt.

Most people who had zero experience with a
baby would have gasped or yelled or held the
baby away from them. Holt didn't do any of those
things. He just stared down at his shirt as if he'd
never seen it before.

Izzy had stopped laughing and was cooing quietly, happy and blissfully unaware that she had
done anything wrong or had probably killed any
last hope that Holt would ever like babies. He
still hadn't looked up and Kathryn moved closer,
ready to scoop Izzy up and offer to clean Holt's
shirt.

He slowly raised his head and chuckled. "You
little booger," he said, but there was no anger in

his tone. "I guess you showed me not to blow raspberries on you. Of course…maybe that means I hurt you. Hell…I mean, heck…I should have known better. What's a rough cowboy like me doing trying to play with somebody as tiny as you are, anyway? You look like you'll break if the wind kicks up a notch. Are you okay?"

Izzy just stared at him with those big blue eyes. She looked at him as if he was an alien life form she wanted to study, as if she was fascinated with this big, deep-voiced creature. Then she blew a wet bubble and made a little fizzy baby sound.

"Is that a no?" he asked.

Kathryn had to smile. "Relax. You didn't hurt her at all," she said, stepping in. "Looks like she did a number on you, though."

"I have other shirts."

"I'll wash that one for you."

"No, you won't. It's fine."

She wrinkled her nose. "Other people might not think so."

"Other people can go straight to…they can just mind their own business."

"She was laughing," Kathryn said. "Really laughing."

"I might have taken the raspberry thing too far."

"She got overly excited. It happens, but she hasn't laughed yet. The books say that's still kind of an advanced skill at her age, and not every baby is there yet. I thought you were going to take her to Johanna."

"I never said that." He stared her down. "I figured I couldn't do too much damage if we didn't move around."

"I was gone a long time. What did you do?"

He shrugged. "We sat and talked."

Kathryn raised an eyebrow.

"I held her on my lap and told her ranch stories. It was pretty boring. She went to sleep. She snored a little."

"I know. It's cute, isn't it?"

He gave her a look. "Don't think I've changed."

"You didn't want to like her."

"I still don't want to like her."

"But you did well."

"I managed. I'm not asking for a gold star."

Izzy was batting at Holt's shirt. Her hand was about to go in the mess. "You better take her." He handed the baby over, rose to his feet, peeled his shirt off. "I hope your interview went okay."

Kathryn tried not to stare at all that bronzed skin and muscle. She hoped she wasn't breathing noticeably faster even though her heartbeat had kicked up. "It did, I think," she said, trying for an airy tone. "I mean, the job is an entry level, but that's to be expected. That's what I want, and it sounds…interesting." But definitely not as interesting as Holt's bare chest or his biceps.

"Well, we should go, Izzy. Thank you so much, Holt."

To her surprise, he smiled. A nice, easy smile. "You're staring, Kathryn."

And she was blushing, too. She was tempted to cover her hot cheeks with her hands, but she was holding Izzy. "Well, yes. Yes, I am. If I took off my blouse, I'm sure you would stare, too."

She had been trying to be bold and a bit audacious, but the steamy, smoky look that Holt gave her…

"Darlin', if you took off your blouse I'd want to do a lot more than look."

With that, he took his stained shirt and turned toward his truck. "I probably shouldn't have said that, but I'm not sorry. It's just the way it is. I'll see you at the fundraiser, Kathryn. I'll have my best host manners on by then." He walked away.

Oh, no, he was not going to make her blush like that and then get the last word, as well. "Make sure you have a shirt on, too," she called.

To her dismay she saw that Luann Dickens was across the street. She was laughing.

"That wasn't the way it sounded," Kathryn said lamely.

"Yes, it was, Luann," Holt said, his voice deadpan.

Luann let out a hoot, Kathryn gave her a frustrated look, and she turned toward home. "That man is…frustrating," she said.

"That's because you want to kiss him," Luann said, close enough now that her voice was much lower. Still, Kathryn turned around to see if Holt had heard.

"He's gone," Luann said. "You can't kiss him now."

But I did want to kiss him again. I wanted to do more than kiss, Kathryn admitted to herself. And it was more than just a physical thing. Holt, despite having his child ripped from him, despite having lost so many people in his life in a few short years that he had to be protecting his heart like mad, had still sacrificed his own fears and feelings to play with Izzy. How could you not love a man like that?

You couldn't. *I do love him,* Kathryn thought. And that was just too damn bad. Because she couldn't have him. She could never have him. Holt, despite being forced into action with Izzy today, was emotionally unavailable. He was un-available in every way and just as off-limits to her now as he had been when she was young. Only then she'd merely had a crush. Now every bit of her longed to be with him. Always.

Too bad. You'll have to settle for your day at the ranch and then hope that a job comes through soon, so you can get out of here before he real-

izes that you've fallen for him. He wouldn't like hurting her. She wasn't going to let him know.

Once she was gone, she would tend to her broken heart.

Alone.

Holt was up long before sunrise on the day of the "Come Be a Cowboy Day." There was so much to do today that he shouldn't have had any time to think, but that didn't stop him. He was, he admitted, seriously messed up.

Kathryn had become too much a part of his life lately. Her parting words to him had him living in a constant state of suppressed desire, her insistence on bravely pushing ahead on this project when he knew that she'd been nervous, and he'd been mean and uncooperative, had won his admiration and…something he didn't want to think about. Her insistence that she and everyone else pay him back for things he'd never expected payback for made him feel something he didn't understand. And that little baby, laughing at him… Kathryn smiling at him…

"Stop it. There's no point in all this." He had

work to do. Kathryn had a life plan that was going to take her to Illinois, or if not Illinois, somewhere else. What would an urban developer do in Larkville once the clinic was done?

Besides, he didn't want her to stay. He didn't want to…feel. Because feeling led to bleakness, pain, loss. He couldn't help remembering the faces of all the people he'd lost these past few years: his parents, Hank, Lilith, the baby… No man would voluntarily step into that kind of hell again. "And I'm not going to," he told Daedalus as he did a final inspection of the barn and corral to make sure they were cleaned up to company standards.

"I believe you." Wes's voice came from Holt's right. "The point is, do you believe you?"

"What are you talking about, Wes?" Holt asked, angry because he'd been caught talking to thin air. "Don't you have something to do?"

Wes held up his hands. He smiled as he backed away. "I've got tons of work. That little gal of yours has given me a whole list. As for what I'm talking about—not a clue. But then you're the one that seemed upset. Something wrong?"

"Yeah. Something's wrong. I've got a whole town full of people and a bunch of tourists showing up here today. Why shouldn't there be something wrong?" Holt asked, grumpier than ever.

Of course, none of those things had anything to do with what was bothering Holt. And he suspected Wes knew it the way the man chuckled as he pulled out his color-coded list and walked away. Everything that was wrong centered around Kathryn.

And everything that was right did, too. What was he going to do about that?

Keep my head down, do my jobs, help her make this day a success and, above all, don't touch her. Don't tell her that she's getting to me. Don't dare do anything that will have her worrying about me once she's gone. Because once she was away from here, he wanted her happy. Blissfully happy with Larkville and him just a fading image in the rearview mirror of that rattletrap car of hers.

CHAPTER FOURTEEN

KATHRYN arrived at the ranch with her heart in her throat. This was a big day in more ways than one. She had received another message from Skyridge already, requesting more information. She might be on the verge of getting a job. That was a good thing, but it also meant that she would be leaving Larkville sooner rather than later.

Suddenly leaving here seemed much more real than it had before. And she wasn't ready. Not just because this time around she'd gotten to know people in Larkville and had made friends, but…

Don't. Don't think of Holt, she ordered herself. If she thought of Holt, she would hurt. And today she had to stand beside him as his hostess. She had to do Larkville and the Double Bar C proud and help win over the benefactors and the doctor candidates. Being sad wasn't allowed.

Taking a deep breath, she pasted on a smile

and removed Izzy from her car seat. "Come on, sweetie. You're going to meet some other babies today. Luann and Mrs. Best have a nursery set up. Let's go find some toys."

Izzy's response was to coo and pat Kathryn's face. She kicked her little feet and then grabbed for the red scarf Kathryn was wearing around her neck. By the time Kathryn had untangled Izzy's fingers, kissing her chubby little fist, they were at the porch. Holt was there, and other people were beginning to spill out the door. To her surprise, Holt took Izzy from her and looked her baby in the eyes as he held her in front of him. "You're lookin' good, Iz," he told her. "Nice…whatever that thing you're wearing is called. That kitten on your tummy is real cute. Play nice with the other kids so your momma won't worry today, okay?"

Izzy wrinkled her nose in her best baby smile. Then she bucked a bit, kicked her tiny feet some more, rounded her lips and made what seemed like a half-formed blowing motion. A bit like the raspberry Holt had given her yesterday. It was probably just a coincidence, probably just an accident, but Holt tilted his head and squinted.

"Yeah, you're your mother's daughter all right. Always asking me to do things. Okay, then. You and me. Later. One raspberry. Maybe two. But no spitting up milk like yesterday, all right? A cowboy needs his dignity." But his voice was gentle as he passed Izzy over to Mrs. Best.

He turned to Kathryn. "Looks like we're all here and everyone has their lists." Was that a smile on his face? If it was, it quickly disappeared as he mentioned to everyone that their guests would be arriving soon. He had flown several groups in last night, and Gus would be bringing them on the bus. "Any last words or last-minute things you want done before we begin?" he asked Kathryn.

She shook her head, trying not to think about how much was riding on this day. "Just…be yourselves. You've made me feel welcome. You all know your skills better than I ever could. Just be prepared to answer a lot of questions, and if you don't know what to say, send them to me or Holt. Depending on what the question is."

"We'll send the men to you and the women to Holt. That should win them over. They'll all leave here in love," Dave, one of Holt's hands, said. He winked at Kathryn, and she laughed.

Holt gave him the evil eye. "The only thing we want them to fall in love with is Larkville and ranch life."

Dave laughed, clearly taking no offense at Holt's cranky tone. "Yes, sir, Holt. We'll show them the best we've got. Ain't that right, boys?" The other men agreed and began to move off to their assigned tasks. Nancy had told Kathryn that the men would walk through fire for Holt just as they would have for his father. There was a mutual respect between the rancher and his cowhands born out of a common background, a love of the land and the sometimes harsh circumstances nature sent their way.

Once everyone was gone, Kathryn looked up at Holt. "Can we walk? I'd like to see Daedalus before the frenzy of the day begins."

To her surprise, he took her hand and she held her breath for a minute, just savoring the feeling of his big palm cupping hers. No doubt she shouldn't indulge herself, but this might be one of the last times she got to do this with him. "I better watch myself," he said. "It wouldn't do for me to get all riled up and grumpy when we have guests. I saw you looking at me that way."

"What way?" For a few seconds, Kathryn's heartbeat started galloping wildly. Did Holt suspect that she had feelings for him beyond simple attraction? Because she would hate for him to know that. When she left here, she wanted to leave proud and tall. Holt's equal, his partner. If he even suspected she was in love with him, he'd get that stern, sad look in his eyes and start telling her what a jerk he was. And that would mean he was trying to let her down easy, that he felt sorry for her. She'd—she would lie to his face and deny she even thought of him as a man before she let that happen, and she hated lies.

Holt was studying her. Waiting. She shook her head. "You managed to get a whole group of people to come here from all over the country. I'm not worried about what they'll think if you get a little grumpy. Most of them will probably fall right in with everyone else and think you're just that cowboy of their imagination, the romantic übermasculine guy with a generous dollop of testosterone in his soul. You being cranky would probably just entrance them more."

He didn't answer. She looked to the side. His lips were twitching.

"I don't believe it. You're laughing at me."

"Sorry, Kathryn, but you sounded just a tad put out that I could behave badly and people would give me a pass because it fits their image of the Hollywood cowboy."

She chuckled. "Well, it seems very unfair that if a woman got grumpy and started giving people deadly looks, no one would sigh and think she was fulfilling some romantic fantasy of theirs. They'd probably give her a wide berth or make insulting and sexist wisecracks."

"No. If it was you, they'd probably be too busy trying to figure out how they could get back in your good graces. You're going to win some hearts today, Kathryn. Dave was right. I'll tell him so. Eventually. I don't want him to get a big head. Not when he's got chores to do. He's leading the bridge crew today. I'm a bit worried about that one and the fencing crew. It seems wrong subjecting people with soft hands and a desire for fun to hard labor."

"I'm not worried. Men who spend their days in suits like getting a chance to pretend they're brawny tough guys who get to swing things, hit things and make things. And everyone here is going to schmooze them to death. We all want good things to happen. I can't imagine anyone walking in here and not feeling welcome."

As they moved toward the corral, Blue followed along, letting Kathryn trail her fingers on his fur. Daedalus whinnied when he saw them, and Kathryn reached in her pocket and pulled out a carrot. Placing it on her palm she held her hand perfectly still until Daedalus took her offering with almost microprecision. "I don't think he would have ever hurt me even that first time. I think you were just mad at me for showing up that day."

"Could be. I have a temper."

"I noticed. It's not an evil temper, though. You turn it on yourself more than you turn it on anyone else. I just tried to corner you that day."

"You *did* corner me. I was stuck with no way

out the minute you made up your mind to begin this project."

"I didn't know it."

He smiled. "I hadn't admitted it at the time, either, but I knew that you were trying to force my hand. And before we begin today, I want to thank you. You've done a good thing, a big thing. I don't know when I've seen everyone here so excited. Today is big doings for a town the size of Larkville. They're beginning to really care about the clinic and to believe it might happen."

"I hope it does. It still might not. It's difficult getting doctors to move to small towns when they can command better money in cities."

"Then I guess we'll just have to offer them something they can't get in a city."

She smiled. "Cowboy charm?" she teased.

He doffed his hat and bowed over her hand. "I aim to please, ma'am." His lips touched her skin, making her feel hot and terribly aware that she was a woman having her hand kissed by the most wanted cowboy in the county.

Just then the bus came down the road and Gus

climbed out and escorted everyone off the vehicle.

"Showtime," Holt said.

"Places," Kathryn agreed. They both made a beeline toward the bus. And with that, "Come Be a Cowboy Day" began.

The ranch was a beehive of activity. Gus was showing the kids the animals. They were chasing chickens, corralling cats and dogs and milking cows. There were craft workshops, roping sessions, work crews. Holt and Kathryn had taken a group of riders out, but it was a large group and each of them had their assigned visitors. Holt knew he might not get a chance to spend any time with her until tonight when all the groups would converge for dinner and a dance.

Instead, he tried to focus on his group. He kept up a running commentary about the ranch and the town and the advantages of being within driving distance from Austin while he watched Kathryn do the same with another subset of the group. She had her head thrown back and she was laughing as she spoke. She looked good on a horse. No one would have known that she had only had one lesson. If he didn't know better, Holt would have wondered if she hadn't whispered some sweet nothings into Daedalus's ear. That horse seemed almost as besotted as the members of her group, both men and women.

"This isn't the way it is most of the time, is it?" a voice asked.

Holt turned to see one of the doctor candidates coming up beside him. "You mean the ranch?"

"The ranch, all of it."

Holt shrugged. "I wouldn't say that. It's just a bit compressed. The way it would be if you made a time-lapse of ranch life. Plus, the weather cooperated and there's no mud, so these are ideal circumstances. You disappointed?" He didn't want to have to tell Kathryn that another candidate was dropping out. One of the three had failed to show up. Now this. Having this man asking such pointed questions had Holt worried, so he might have sounded just a bit cranky in spite of his promise to tone it down.

"Am I disappointed?" the man asked. "Nope. Just making sure I know as much as possible. I've spoken with Dr. Cooper, of course. Ms. Ellis put me in touch with him, and he's given me a good idea of what his practice entails, but anyone who signs on to take the job—if it's offered—will have to live here."

"It's a good place," Holt said.

"Ms. Ellis said that, too. I'd really like to get to know her better."

"She's not part of the package."

"I—"

Dammit, why had he put it that way? "By that I merely meant that she's planning to move away very soon."

The man didn't answer, and Holt glanced toward him. To his surprise, the guy, Lee Sullivan, was smiling. "You have a thing for her, don't you?"

No. No. No. Yes, of course. Who wouldn't? "It's not like that."

"Which probably means, 'Mind your own business.' I don't blame you. I'm half in love with her myself and I've barely met her."

Half in love with her. Half in love with her. The words skimmed through Holt's mind the rest of the day. It wasn't as if he hadn't already thought the same thing and pushed it aside. It was just that this day, that guy, her job situation, all served to keep Kathryn's impending departure on his mind constantly. He dreaded having to say goodbye, and he hated that he even cared. But that couldn't matter. He had spent a lifetime submerging his emotions. He wasn't going to let them start leading him around now. Especially not when it would upset Kathryn to know that his interest in her was more than merely physical. And way more than merely friendship.

With the greatest of effort, he tamped all of that down. And waited for the night when he hoped he could dance with her. Getting close to her might be difficult in this crowd of admiring males.

Kathryn had cleaned up and changed into a white blouse and a blue skirt with a bandanna at her throat. She still had several hours of being on camera, of having to woo people, and all she wanted was some time to spend with Holt.

That was wrong. This was something she had started and it was important. Under ordinary circumstances she would be happy. The day had been going great once she'd accepted the fact that they were down to only two doctor candidates. But when she had turned on her cell phone that had been turned off, she found a message. Ed Austen's voice said, "Congratulations! The job is yours if you want it. Come out Monday? We'll put you and your daughter up in temporary housing until you can find your own place. Call me."

She hadn't called. Not yet. And she hadn't told Holt. This day was for Larkville and for him. This day was to be their first triumph. She wasn't going to inject her own personal plans into it.

And the truth was, she didn't want to think about leaving Holt. Not today. Instead, she found her smile. She entered the room where Ellie Jackson was giving everyone dance lessons. Ellie was a former ballet dancer from New York, and while ballet might be her usual game, she clearly knew her Texas two-step, too.

Kathryn found a place near the back of the room and within seconds Holt was there. Her chest, which had been fine all day, felt suddenly tight. "You want a progress report?" she asked.

"Only if you want to give me one. What I want is a dance partner."

"I'm afraid I'm not very good at this."

"That's why you have Ellie. And me." And he swirled her into his arms and into the dance. She stumbled. "Easy," he said, his hands on her to stabilize her. "It's a triple step, then another, then two singles. That's right. We're just going to keep it simple at first. We'll dress it up when you're comfortable."

"Holt?"

"Yes?" His palm was at her waist, the warmth of his touch seeping through to her skin. She felt flushed and achy. Surely anyone could see how he was affecting her.

"I may never get comfortable," she said. Not with him holding her. But then he was twirling her, guiding her and she fit with him, moved with him. He moved toward her, he turned her in his arms. And she followed as if she had been dancing with him all her life.

"Hot. Very hot," Luann said as she glided past, her duties with the little ones turned over to Mrs.

Best. Kathryn couldn't have agreed more. She felt very hot, and perfect.

"Okay, a dip, just for fun," Holt said, and he dipped her back over his arm at the end of the song. His face was over hers, his lips were so close. She was… Oh, my word, she had been reaching out to pull him even closer. Instantly, she scrambled and nearly fell. Holt righted her immediately.

"May I cut in?" one of the benefactors asked. "I can't promise you anything like that, but I won't embarrass you too much, I don't think." He was an older man, a very nice man who had lost his wife and who was still sad.

Immediately Holt and Kathryn separated. She smiled at the man even as she was completely aware of Holt moving away from her. Asking other women to dance. And she accepted dances from other men. That was the way the rest of the evening went.

And this was how the rest of her life would go. She and Holt had had their time, and now she had a job. They would both move on. Their time together was over.

* * *

Could a man be more frustrated than he was right now? On the one hand he should be ecstatic. The young doctor from the trail seemed interested in the town and maybe the job, they had raised a lot of money and everyone had had a good time. But every time he had tried to get close to Kathryn, some other man had stepped in to take his place. And he'd had to let him. Them. All of them.

After that first dance, he hadn't gotten close to her again and now she was standing in front of him telling him…

"I'm going home on the bus with Gus."

He blinked. "I can drive you."

She shook her head. "No."

"You want to explain that? Have I been channeling that jackass husband the way I've done so often with you? Made you angry? Pushed you?" Wasn't he pushing her now by asking all these stupid questions that were really none of his business?

Again, she shook her head. She looked tired. He felt like a beast for prodding her. "No, I just… I have to think, and I don't trust myself to think straight with you there. You make me want to do risky, unwise things."

"And you don't like that."

"I like that too well, but tonight I can't. I have to return a phone call. From Illinois."

Then she was gone, and he didn't know whether the phone call had been good news or bad. It had been obvious that she wasn't in a sharing mood. She was withholding crucial information from him. And it was her right. This wasn't like Lilith. This was Kathryn, and she had every right to tell him nothing at all if she so desired.

And there wasn't a thing he could do about it, was there?

CHAPTER FIFTEEN

KATHRYN looked around her at her little house and tried to decide what she should do. She had asked Mrs. Best to take Izzy, but she hadn't told her why she needed time to be alone.

In truth, there wasn't a good reason. She had called Ed Austen; she had done the only thing she could do. By rights she should be ecstatic.

And I will be, she promised herself. This was what she had set out to do. Get a job in her field. Become independent. Make her own little family. It was perfect.

Except…

When the knock came at the door, she knew it was Holt. She had been less than forthcoming with him last night. Because she was afraid she might do something stupid. Like cry. Or get clingy. She'd been tired and not completely in control of her emotions. There had been a very good chance that she might have done something emotional, something they'd both regret.

But it was morning now. She should be fine. Had to be fine.

She opened the door. And looked up into those dark eyes. She wasn't fine.

"I just came by to…see how you thought everything went yesterday."

Kathryn nodded. She wanted to sock him on the arm. He was so obviously making that up. "It went well. Fantastic. Don't you think?"

"Me? Yeah. Great. I think we'll probably bag that young doctor. And we pulled in enough… I've got some architects in mind and—hell, Kathryn. I don't want to talk about the clinic."

She waited.

"The phone call," he said. "Yes or no?"

"Yes." Her voice sounded too weak. "Yes," she tried again. "I start Monday."

He let out a whistle. It sounded very nonchalant. Her heart felt very rocklike. She wanted to kick some of the piles of stuff she had been trying to organize and sort for the trip. "Monday?"

"I couldn't say no. It's a good opportunity."

"Yes, it is. I'm happy for you. You can do and be all those things you wanted to."

"I know. Isn't it great?" She tried so very hard to dredge up a brilliant smile and a convincing tone of voice. The last thing she wanted was for Holt to know that when she left here she left… in love with him. This was a man who piled responsibility on himself. She didn't want him to feel responsible for her. Or to feel guilty when he heard her name. *Light. Keep it light,* she ordered herself.

"I'm going to miss all the good stuff, the plans for the clinic, the groundbreaking," she told him, trying to keep her smile brilliant. "Send me— send me lists."

"Right. Sure thing."

She had motioned him to the couch. Now she stared down at him. "You're not going to, are you?" And why should he? He didn't owe her anything. She shouldn't even want him to contact her. It would only open the wound over and over.

"I—Kathryn, no, I'm not going to send you lists or anything else," he said, shaking his head.

"When things end, they're done. I don't look back."

That felt like a blow, and yet she tried to put herself in his place. He'd faced so much. A weaker man might have gone crazy.

"I shouldn't ask, but is that because…I know you've lost a lot of loved ones…"

"No point in remembering."

"Even the good memories?" She didn't wait for him to answer. "Holt, I want to be a good memory. Someone who makes you smile when you think about her. You say that you're not a sensitive or emotional man. But I've seen how patient you are with Mrs. Best and how mad you were when Ava DuShay's son wasn't treating her right. You may have a responsibility to the people of Larkville, but all those things you… I'm just not buying that it's all out of duty or that you're some emotionless robot. You care what happens to people. They touch your heart even if you don't say the words. Why do the words matter? You show them instead. So don't put me on your 'do not remember' list. Remember me just a little. We've been friends, haven't we?"

He reached up and took her hand, pulling her

down beside him on the couch. "Don't you ever give up?"

"Yes. Yes I do. Sometimes, but—"

"Shh." He drew her onto his lap. He kissed her, a long, sweet kiss. "Don't you want to know what I'm doing?" he asked.

"You're kissing me. I'm kissing you, too."

"I'm making some good memories," he whispered against her mouth.

She smiled against his lips. Her heart was still filled with pain, but she wove her way around it, over it, under it. The pain would wait. Now she was with Holt. "Let's make more memories," she said. "Izzy is at Mrs. Best's."

"We're alone? No one's going to cut in and ask you to dance?"

"Just you. Dancing with me. We'll begin where we left off last night. Where was it?"

"I think it was…here," he said, sliding his palm around her back. "And then here." He gently touched her lips.

"And this was where we were headed," she whispered, and she leaned into him, kissing him more deeply. She placed her palms on his shirt. "Open the buttons for me."

He never stopped kissing her, but in seconds she was able to push his shirt wide. He slithered out of it.

"We could dance better, closer, without these," he said, removing her blouse and then her jeans. As he turned with her, rolled with her, danced with her, they did away with the rest of their clothes. Then he took her in his arms and danced her into her bedroom. He laid her on the mattress, he braced himself above her. "When you're gone, I'll send you whatever you ask for," he whispered.

"Send me you. Now," she said.

"With pleasure," he agreed.

And he was right. Kathryn had never been loved so well. She knew why, too.

Because Holt knew how to love in many ways even if he didn't actually love her. And also because she actually *did* love him. Desperately. Hopelessly. Now wasn't the time to think about or regret that. She would have a lifetime to get over loving Holt.

She didn't hesitate. She had no desire to hold back, because these would be her last memories of him. She wanted them to be perfect.

So when they finally awoke, she kissed him once more, loving him with all her heart. "Don't stay," she said. "I have to get ready. I have to pack and leave."

Within moments he was gone. Forever. Only the thought that she had a child to take care of kept her from collapsing.

Holt rode Daedalus for miles. And then for more miles. He paid no attention to time or the weather. He could have ridden forever but a man's horse shouldn't have to bear the grief of the man.

Eventually, he came back and stopped by the creek. This had always been one of his favorite places. Today it was empty, and his heart wasn't here.

"She's almost gone, boy. You won't see her again and neither will I," he said. "I wish I had some way to change things so that what she needs and wants could be here. I wish I had the words to make her want to stay, but that's never been me. Not good with words or matters of the heart. Lots of disappointed people, lots of loss. People think I'm something because of the Double

Bar C, but I'm not so much. Kathryn, now, she's something. She knows how to get things done, how to make people want to do the things she wants. Her and her lists." Those silly, sweet lists. She drove him mad with them. She made him smile.

If he hadn't been in so much pain, he might have smiled now. As it was, smiling wasn't an option today.

He hadn't even said a word when he left last night, the last time he would ever speak to her.

Don't feel, he remembered his father saying in a rare moment of introspection. *Feeling makes you weak and brings you trouble. Don't ever say anything that will let anyone see into your soul and give them power over you. Just work. Love comes and goes, but the ranch is a lasting legacy. That's all that matters in life.*

Don't you dare cry, Clay had said when he got hurt.

Pick yourself up and move on, his father had said when his dog died. *Don't feel. Don't feel. Don't let yourself be blinded by passion.* The words echoed through his mind.

Holt got up and began trying to outwalk the litany running through his head. *Don't feel. Don't feel.* He'd followed that directive all his life. It had crippled him to the point where his throat froze every time he even thought the word *love*.

But I love her. Holt lurched, bumping into Daedalus, who sidestepped and whinnied.

"Sorry, boy," Holt said. "Look what I did. Just thinking the words messed me up. How could I ever tell her?"

Maybe he didn't have to. The thought came to him in all capitals, in bold. What had Kathryn said? That the words weren't important because she knew that he cared about people?

Maybe so, but that seems way too easy. That's like giving me a pass to be a total jerk.

Besides, for the first time in his memory, he *wanted* to love and to say the words. He wanted to let his heart out of its cage and be able to tell the woman he loved that he cared. And not awkwardly, either. Kathryn was a woman who liked words, no matter what she'd said. Otherwise, she wouldn't work for a newspaper and fill up reams of paper with her lists.

You'll mess it up. You'll say the wrong thing. You might even yell and act stupid. And what's the point, anyway? She's going. She's going.

And maybe that was the point exactly. She was going without knowing that she was loved beyond belief. She wanted him to have good memories of her? He wanted her to know that she had changed him in a way no one ever had before. He wanted her to know how much she mattered, to give her what all the people she'd loved had withheld from her. Too bad he wasn't an eloquent man.

Still, he intended to make the effort.

Kathryn was crossing the park on her way to the SmartMart. She needed some last-minute items to tide Izzy over for the trip and her mind was so…no, it was her *heart* that was the problem. She kept forgetting things.

But this was absolutely the last trip to the store. She had her bags in the car, she'd said her goodbyes to everyone in town and there was nothing left to do but go. And try to get over Holt. Because she hurt. She was a mess.

You shouldn't have trusted him. The thought

slid in. *He hurt you the way everyone else has.* But no, that wasn't true. He had warned her from the first that he wasn't a man a woman should love. He had tried to protect her heart, and everything he did, everything he was, was honorable. He was the most trustworthy man she knew. He had given her back what she had lost: trust, faith in herself and in others. It wasn't his fault that he didn't love her the way she loved him.

Stop thinking. Stop feeling. Go, she told herself. So, she got the things she needed from the store, she put them in the car and put Izzy in her car seat. She took one last look around and turned to go, fighting the tears in her throat. She reached for the car door handle. *Go. Go now before you break down right here in public.*

"Kathryn, don't. Don't go." Holt's voice sounded behind her and she whirled, almost into his arms. "Don't go *yet,*" he clarified.

"What's wrong?" There had to be something wrong. He had left hours ago, and Holt was, as he'd said, a man who never looked back.

"I lied," he said. "I *do* look back. I *do* remember. And I regret. I think of the things I wish I'd said, and you'd think that would help me the next time, but it doesn't. So I live with the fact that my father and I never shared our feelings, I probably didn't give my friend Hank the proper goodbye he needed and if I had been able to tell Lilith what she wanted to hear, our child…well, I don't know, but maybe the ending might have felt less brutal. Now here you are, and you matter… the most. I can say the unimportant things, the grumpy things, I can discuss minor issues, I can even offer you mundane compliments. But to express what's in here—" he tapped his chest "—it's awkward, dumb, not anything anyone would want to hear."

For a second she started to say that she would, but that might sound as if she was pressuring him. "Holt, when I came here I didn't trust anyone, not even myself. I was running scared and bluffing my way through, trying to look capable so no one would see how frightened and unsure I was. Everyone I had cared about had betrayed me and criticized me. And then there was you. You didn't sugarcoat anything and you didn't even cooperate half the time, but you were true. You had your principles and your rules and you stuck to them no matter what. You were—*are*—the most trustworthy man I've ever met. Knowing that you existed, that there was one solid, steadfast person in the world I could depend on, come flood or fire, changed me, inspired me to have faith in myself and helped me become more than I'd ever been. So there's nothing you could ever say that I wouldn't want to hear, no matter how awkwardly it was phrased. But I want you to know that you don't have to say anything."

"Kathryn. Hell, Kathryn, I didn't even say thank you for last night."

Her heart lurched. She managed a smile. "Yes, you did. You didn't have to say the words. You *showed* me." And then she just couldn't help herself. She rose on her toes and kissed him. Just once.

He groaned. He kissed her, too. Just once. Then, reaching into his pocket, he pulled out a folded sheet of paper. He handed it to her and she unfolded it. It was color-coded.

The code for *Physical* was yellow.

You make my knees weak. I wake up every

morning wanting to kiss you; I go to sleep each night wanting to hold you. The scent of your hair makes me think of…sunshine and fields of roses. When you grow old, I'll still love looking at you, because your beauty comes from the inside.

She didn't read it out loud because she could already see that Holt was squirming under her scrutiny of his prose. She moved on to blue for *Other.*

You make me want to be a better man than I am. You drive me crazy with your demands, but I seem to like being driven crazy because I look forward to seeing you. Every day. You have a beautiful, sweet baby girl I adore.

Kathryn had to stop reading for a minute while she wiped her eyes. Then she looked down again. There was just one thing more.

I am so happy for your success. I want you to be happy forever, and I want you to know that I will love you all the days of my life.

Her face nearly crumpled. "For real?" she asked.

"It's on the list, isn't it?" he asked, drawing her to him and whispering against her neck. "Lists don't lie. At least ours don't."

"I liked the color-coding."

"Two seemed kind of skimpy, but I was afraid you would leave before I finished. Besides, this was my first time. I don't have any practice in writing love letters."

"I'm glad. I wouldn't want to think of some other woman reading about how you love her."

"That won't happen. You're the one, the only one. All the days of my life," he repeated. "Now. What time do you have to be in Illinois?" His voice sounded thick.

"You're not asking me to stay?"

He hesitated. "I don't want to stand in your way. You worked hard to get your degree and to get this job."

"And I'll get another one. Closer to home. Closer to Larkville. Austin's close. If I make a big enough nuisance of myself, maybe they'll like me and give me a job."

"Maybe they'll love you," he said, and he kissed her nose and then her lips.

"Just as long as you do."

"I definitely do love you, Kathryn."

"Do you want to know how much I love you, Holt?"

"I hope it's a lot. I hope you'll agree to marry me."

"I think it was written in the cards. Or at least it was written." She reached into her purse and pulled out a folded piece of paper. "When I was cleaning out boxes for packing today, I came across this. It was written years ago and I was pretty young, so I'm sorry for the girlish cursive and the purple ink."

She opened the yellowing sheet of paper where a much younger Kathryn had written "I love, love, love, love, love…"

The words went to the end of the page where Holt's name was printed. And in the header of the paper, she had written "Kathryn Calhoun. Mrs. Holt Calhoun."

"How could I not marry you?" she teased. "It

says right here in bright purple that my name is Kathryn Calhoun."

He laughed out loud. "Darlin', how did I miss you back then?" he asked.

"It doesn't matter. You've got me now."

And he swept her into his arms. He had her.

EPILOGUE

ON a sunny blue-sky day in August, three months after Kathryn had walked back into Holt's world, Kathryn and Holt embarked on their next project together: their wedding. The Double Bar C had never looked so festive. There were white and pale blue ribbons and flowers everywhere. Daedalus even had pale blue ribbons braided into his mane as Kathryn, dressed in a white dress and perched precariously on a sidesaddle, met Holt at the juncture where they were to begin the procession.

As he mounted his father's stallion, Storm, he smiled at her. "I hope you know that only the fact that I love you more than I love my dignity or my horse's dignity is getting me up on a horse that is decked out in ribbons."

Kathryn's heart filled to overflowing. "I hope *you* know that I love you enough that I would have married you in a mud hut with no ribbons, flowers or guests."

"I do," he said. "But I want people to know how much I care. You deserve only the best."

"Well, I've got the best. The best cowboy. The best man."

"Ah, I see you're still delusional, love. Well, let's ride, then." They turned their horses in the direction of their eager audience.

The people of Larkville lined a rose-petal-strewn path that led to an altar at the edge of a grassy field. They cheered as Holt and Kathryn passed by.

When the two of them reached the altar, Wes and Dave led the horses away, and Holt turned to Kathryn. He kissed her.

"Not yet," someone shouted and everyone laughed.

"I love you," he said.

"Not yet for that, either," someone else said.

Kathryn kissed Holt. "I love *you*."

"Would someone please get these two married already?" a third person called out.

So the ceremony began. It was short and sweet

with the only holdup being when Blue delivered the rings and wanted to lick Kathryn to death. The pastor had barely said the last words before Holt swept Kathryn close. "Thank you for waiting for me," he said, as his mouth covered hers in a kiss that took Kathryn's breath away. Then he kissed her again, softer this time. Sweeter, but just as nice. All Holt's kisses were nice.

Eventually, however, he set her back on her feet, and they smiled at each other as the recessional music began.

Holt held his arm out to Kathryn, but she shook her head. "Not yet," she said quietly. "Gus?"

Gus, who was seated in the front row, stepped forward. He was holding a book.

Holt raised an eyebrow. "You want me to read? Now?"

Kathryn took the book. "Not exactly. I just… Remember the day everyone was giving you gifts and you wouldn't take mine? This is it. I researched the history of the Double Bar C, and everyone contributed photographs and stories. It's made so you can add more pages. Things about your parents and Jess, Megan and Nate only you would know. And your new brothers and sisters." She smiled at Ellie, who smiled back.

Holt looked down. He blinked. Then he took Kathryn's face in both his hands and kissed her, hard. He smiled at his sisters, who were beaming, and at Nate, recently home from the army, who gave him a silent nod. Then he turned to Ellie. "I would love to know more. To know *you*. All of you."

Ellie blinked back tears. "I'm going to love getting to know you, too."

In the brief moment that followed, Kathryn leaned toward Holt and whispered, "I didn't want to put anything about your baby or Lilith in there without talking to you, but I want you to know that he—or she—is going in there. I know you wanted that baby and grieved its loss."

Holt didn't speak for a minute. When he did, his voice was thick. "Thank you. I *did* love that baby and I hope you know that I love Izzy heart and soul. I consider her mine."

She smiled. "You're going to be such a good daddy if you don't spoil her silly. She already adores you."

He grinned. "I intend to spoil all our children silly. I mean to love them like crazy and tell them so every day, but I'm never going to love anyone the way that I love you."

"We can't hear you," someone yelled. "What are you talking about?"

Holt and Kathryn turned to face all of Larkville. "We're talking about making babies. Kathryn wants to get right on it," Holt said.

"Now?" Wes asked, laughing.

"Just as soon as Holt quits talking," Kathryn teased. "This man just loves to talk and make long speeches."

Everyone laughed, and Holt smiled at his wife. "You're going to pay for that, darlin'."

"I certainly hope so, love," she said. "Here's my first payment." And she launched herself into his arms.

The people of Larkville went wild. Holt Calhoun had finally found his voice, his love, his future and his reason for living.

* * * * *